Her Sleigh Ride Christmas Cowboy

Big Sky Christmas, Book 4

Jenna Hendricks

Copyright

This book is a work of fiction. All of the characters, organizations, and events portrayed in this novel are either products of the author's imagination or are used fictitiously.

Copyright (c) 2021 Jenna Hendricks

All rights reserved. No part of this publication may be reproduced, stored in a retrieval system, or transmitted in any form or by any means, electronic, mechanical, recording or otherwise, without the prior written permission of the author. Please purchase only authorized electronic editions, and do not participate in or encourage electronic piracy of copyrighted materials.

This ebook is licensed for your personal enjoyment only. It may not be sold or given away to other people. If you would like to share this book with another person, please purchase an additional copy for each recipient. If you are reading this book and did not purchase it, or it was not purchased for your use only, then please purchase your own copy.

Cover Design by Victoria Cooper

First Edition October 2021

All rights reserved. Copyright © 2021 Jenna Hendricks

Contents

Books by Jenna Hendricks

Triple J Ranch –

Book 0 - Finding Love in Montana (Join my newsletter to get this book for free)

Book 1 - Second Chance Ranch – also available on audio

Book 2 – Cowboy Ranch – also available on audio

Book 3 – Runaway Cowgirl Bride

Book 4 – Faith of A Cowboy

Book 5 – Cowboy Blessings

Book 6 – The Cowboy's Game

Big Sky Christmas –

Book 1 – Her Montana Christmas Cowboy

Book 2 – Her Christmas Rodeo Cowboy

Book 3 – Her Mistletoe Cowboy

Book 4 – Her Sleigh Ride Christmas Cowboy

Crooked Arrow Ranch-

Book 1 – A Broken Heart Mended

Book 2 – Hope's Healing Love

Book 3 - Love's Healing Balm

Standalone books –

Christmas Crazy In July

See these titles and more: https://JennaHendricks.com

Other Books by J.L. Hendricks (my 1st pen name)

New Orleans Magic

Book 0.5: Magic's Not Real

Book 1: New Orleans Magic

Book 2: Hurricane of Magic

Book 3: Council of Magic

Worlds Away Series

Book 0: Worlds Revealed (join my Newsletter to get this exclusive freebie)

Book 1: Worlds Away

Book 2: Worlds Collide

Book 2.5: Worlds Explode

Book 3: Worlds Entwined

A Shifter Christmas Romance Series

Book 0: Santa Meets Mrs. Claus

Book 1: Miss Claus and the Secret Santa

Book 2: Miss Claus under the Mistletoe

Book 3: Miss Claus and the Christmas Wedding

Book 4: Miss Claus and Her Polar Opposite

The FBI Dragon Chronicles

Book 1: A Ritual of Fire

Book 2: A Ritual of Death

Book 3: A Ritual of Conquest

Chronicles of the Unwanted Princess

Book 1: The Portal of Chance

Book 2: The Forbidden Portal

Book 3: The Emerald Portal

Misfit Island

Prequel: Island of Misfits

See these titles and more at https://www.jlhendricksauthor.com/

Newsletter Sign-up

By signing up for my newsletter, you will get a free copy of the prequel to the Triple J Ranch series, Finding Love in Montana. As well as another free book from J.L. Hendricks.

And for a limited time, the prequel to the new Crooked Arrow Ranch series, Wounded Hearts, will also be included.

If you want to make sure you hear about the latest and greatest, sign up for my newsletter at: Subscribe to Jenna Hendricks' newsletter. I will only send out a few e-mails a month. I'll do cover reveals, snippets of new books, and giveaways or promos in the newsletter, some of which will only be available to newsletter subscribers. https://jennahendricks.com/newsletter/

JENNA HENDRICKS
TRIPLE J RANCH
Finding Love in Montana
A Triple J Ranch Prequel

This book is dedicated to all of our men and women who have served, and will serve, our great nation. We may not always agree on politics or even military decisions, but I will always support you in any way I can.
None of you will ever be forgotten.
All Americans should thank you for your service, no matter when you served. We, as well as most of the world, owe our freedom to those who served before us.
The world would be a much scarier place if the US Military hadn't joined in the fight for WWI and WWII.
And for those who came home injured, please know that you are loved and prayed for.

M egan had to do a double take on Main Street. Was that a costume, or was the prince of England here for the Frenchtown Halloween celebration?

"Megan, slow down," Sam Marley grumbled as he followed her toward who knew what.

Behind them were Mike and Skeeter, two of the Crooked Arrow Ranch's guests and some of the nicest guys Megan had ever worked with. She knew they'd be alright if she got a little bit ahead of them; it wasn't like Frenchtown was so large you could get lost.

Well, not on most days. To be fair, it was pretty busy right then. The town's annual Halloween pageant was slowly meandering down Main Street. The area children, all dressed up in their cute little Halloween costumes, starred in this parade along with their parents.

Megan chuckled at the sight of a man dressed as a pirate with his pirate pig at his side. She wasn't sure if the pig was normally pink with black patches all over, or if the owner had painted the pig that way. The poor little pot-bellied pig was even wearing a pirate patch over one eye. It was more than adorable.

When she paused, Sam caught up to her, breathing hard. "Megan, you gotta go slower fer us. Not all of us has the ability to walk fast." He looked back at Skeeter and frowned.

Skeeter Murphy was having difficulty hobbling along with his crutches. The poor Army veteran had almost lost his legs to a roadside bomb in Afghanistan. Thankfully, the Army doctors were able to save his legs. Now he had a long road to recovery, which included using crutches for a few more months.

When Megan looked back and saw Skeeter wobbling and sweating—even though it wasn't even close to being hot outside, not with the recent snowstorms—she immediately felt contrite and bit her lower lip. She raised an arm and waved to Skeeter. "Sorry, buddy."

Of all people at the Crooked Arrow Ranch, where they all lived, she knew better than to push any of the disabled vets so hard they almost fell. Megan was a counselor who specialized in treating war veterans suffering from PTSD. She'd only been at the ranch a few months, but it was exactly where she belonged, and she knew it.

The other man in their party, Mike Blankenship, wasn't physically disabled. No, his injuries went much deeper than what anyone could see with their eyes. Megan wasn't sure what had happened to him, but she did know that he had seen too much evil to come home whole. The man was very quiet until it came to talking about the cows, and his butter. Mike loved to make butter and cream and anything else he could from the milk he extracted every day from the cows he loved and cared for. Then, you couldn't get him to shut up.

"Sorry guys, I thought I saw the strangest sight." Megan shook her head. "But it couldn't be." She took her hat off and rubbed her forehead while scanning the crowd for the man she had noticed earlier.

"Oh, you mean Pirate Spot?" Sam grinned.

"Huh?" Megan furrowed her brow and her nose scrunched as though she had smelled rotten pumpkins.

"The tiny pig that looks like a pirate." Skeeter pointed to the pig, who was farther away than when Megan first noticed it.

She shook her head. "No, not the pig." Megan looked at Sam. "His name is Pirate Spot? Really? Does he always look like that?"

All three men nodded in unison. "Yes, ma'am."

"Huh, that's interesting." She looked back down the street and watched as the tiny pig seemed to dance his way down the road. "He's so cute."

"The pig, or his owner?" Sam waggled his brows and barked out a laugh. The man rarely laughed unless it was at his own jokes.

"The pig." Megan glared at Sam.

"Well now Miss Megan, I do think that label can apply to men as well as actual swine." Skeeter's open-mouthed smile showed off his pearly whites. The man was outgoing and good-looking, if not a bit cheeky at times.

Megan rolled her eyes. "And how much longer are you with us?"

The two of them bantered back and forth as though they were brother and sister and not counselor and patient. Megan doubted Skeeter ever treated his medical team like doctors. She guessed he'd flirted with all the nurses while staying in the hospital after surviving the attack on his convoy. She also knew he didn't suffer much from PTSD, but he was going to have a permanent issue with both of his legs, and that was why he was at the ranch.

"No, that's not what I was looking at, as cute as the swine is. I thought I saw a celebrity, but it couldn't be. Not here in Frenchtown, Montana." Megan laughed at herself for thinking she'd seen the younger prince from the royal family. Sure, he lived in the US now, but the prince was out in California, not Montana.

Then she saw a lock of red hair out of the corner of her eye and turned to see if it might be him.

"Look"—Skeeter pointed past the kids in the parade—"there's the Rock!"

Megan and her group turned to where Skeeter was pointing. "Where? I don't see Dwayne Johnson."

Sam guffawed. "Oh, I see the rock alright."

Megan turned confused eyes on Sam. "Where?"

Sam pointed to a boulder next to the sports store where they sold rock-climbing equipment.

All eyes glared at Skeeter.

"Really?" Megan pursed her lips and shook her head. Then went back to scanning the crowd for that red hair.

"What? You said you saw a celebrity and I said I saw a rock." His face was all innocence. However, Skeeter was anything but innocent. The man was a smooth operator. With his good looks and sanguine personality, he'd have all the women of Frenchtown falling over themselves to get his attention in no time.

Even with two busted legs.

Well, his good looks weren't exactly shining at the moment. Skeeter wasn't too tall; he was about five feet ten inches. And his black hair was thick and had a natural wave to it. When he was clean-shaven, he looked like an angel. However, for the winter he had decided to go all mountain man and he sported a scraggly beard that needed more than just a good trim. If Megan wasn't mistaken, he was also keeping snacks in that awful beard of his.

It was a few minutes later when she saw *him* and her feet automatically went in his direction. The man was good-looking with his ginger-red hair that now had a hat on top of it. For a moment she thought this couldn't be the man she had seen earlier, as he hadn't had a Stetson on when she'd first noticed him. But as she continued to scan him up and down, she realized this was the man who caught her attention. And he did resemble a cowboy version of Prince Harry with his thick ginger hair and a smile that could make any woman weak in the knees.

This cowboy had on faded denim jeans that fit him loosely through the legs. When she noticed his shiny belt buckle, she realized his jeans fit like a glove around his hips. Not wanting to look where she shouldn't, she raised her roaming eyes up his torso. He had on a thick Carhartt tan jacket that was zipped up, and his Stetson was the same shade of tan. The brim covered his face at first, until he turned and looked directly at her. Then she noticed his brilliant blue-gray eyes, just like Prince Harry's.

When he noticed her staring at him, he grinned. Then he checked her out in a very obvious way that left Megan feeling light-headed. Before she could move, he winked at her. That was enough to turn her stomach sour. The man wasn't Prince Harry, but he acted as though he was just as good as a prince. That kind of man always turned her off.

Megan scoffed and turned the other direction. "Come on, guys. Let's get going. We've gotta pick up those supplies and head back to the ranch before we miss dinner."

Chapter 2

D aniel Caruthers loved attending the events in town for all holidays. But there was something about Halloween. Maybe because it was the last holiday before his super-busy season began? Or maybe it was the fact that everything was pumpkin flavored. His favorite day this year was when Lottie Hamilton started selling her famous pumpkin spice lattes. Yes, he knew it was a froufrou drink that women adored, but who said men couldn't enjoy it?

In fact, he was just exiting the famous Frenchtown Roasting Company with a PSL in one hand and the last two bites of Lottie's outstanding pumpkin scone in the other. Daniel knew that his boss, Cody Makinaw, loved the new huckleberry scones that Sadie McKinley made, and they were good, but nothing was as tasty as the pumpkin scone in his mouth. Not only could he taste the sweet pumpkin, but there was also a hint of cinnamon and nutmeg that sent his tastebuds bucking for more than seven seconds. Not to mention the cinnamon drizzle on top.

He'd never admit it to anyone, but Daniel could easily eat a whole batch of the cinnamon drizzle and still want several pumpkin scones. Not that he'd ever tried it, but…

He stood there on the walkway outside the coffee shop, grinning while he finished up his pumpkin treat. The kids from

Frenchtown and the surrounding ranches were all dressed up in their favorite costumes, parading down the street. He saw a cute little mermaid with her homemade tail trailing behind her. Then he grinned at two young boys in firemen costumes at least three sizes too big. But his favorite costumes in the parade were always the pets'.

Not only had Malachi brought his pirate pig, but the Miller boy had his dog with him. They were both dressed up as dinosaurs. Buddy's dog looked like a stegosaurus, but Daniel wasn't too sure if he'd gotten the name right. The dog's costume took advantage of his four legs and tall back, which sported two-inch-thick plates standing up all along it and down the tail. They moved as though they didn't weigh much, easily blowing in the breeze, so Daniel figured they were made out of foam or something just as light.

And Buddy, who was about ten years old, was rocking his T-Rex costume. All boys who went to school in Montana knew that the first T-Rex was discovered in Montana, so that was always the favorite dinosaur. Even Daniel loved the T-Rex when he was a boy. Oh, who was he kidding, he still loved the giant carnivore. And that was always the first fossil he looked for whenever he went to a museum.

Instead of standing there all alone, Daniel decided to head out into the crowds and see if he could find any of his friends. He knew his boss wouldn't be there. Cody was a workaholic who didn't know what the word "fun" meant anymore.

So when he discovered Cody watching the parade, he almost dropped the last of his PSL. Instead, he finished it off and tossed the cup in the trash before heading over to hassle his boss for having some fun.

"Cody, are you actually having fun?" It wasn't that Daniel didn't think his boss knew what fun was, but he had rarely seen him have fun in the past decade.

A chortle escaped Cody and he smiled at his employee. "You know, I do go out and have fun. It's just that my version of fun is different from yours."

Daniel bent over laughing. Cody's joke wasn't that funny, but the fact that his boss thought he knew how to have fun? *That* was funny. "Since when?"

"Hey now," Cody chided.

Instead of getting himself in trouble, Daniel began looking for the woman Cody had come to town to find. Instead, he found someone much more interesting.

When he discovered a vision of loveliness checking him out, he couldn't help but look her up and down as well. A whistle built up behind his lips, but he halted that impulse immediately. Daniel had recently learned that women didn't like it when strangers whistled at them. He didn't mean any disrespect—on the contrary, he only wanted to show his appreciation for a pretty girl.

However, he did give a cocky wink without realizing it. She gave him a look of disgust. Too bad, because she was beautiful. Even with cowboy boots on, the lady wasn't quite as tall as he was, and her sandy brown hair fell around her face and down her back. Long hair was one of those feminine attributes that made Daniel's fingers itch. He loved to run his fingers through long, silky hair. But he rarely did it.

Daniel loved women, but he also respected them and knew he didn't want to lead anyone on or give them the wrong impression. Sure, he enjoyed flirting with a pretty cowgirl just like the next guy, but also knew that if he wasn't careful he'd end up making a huge mistake. He'd seen too many high school and college buddies get their girlfriends pregnant only to have to marry them. Most of them were now divorced or going through a divorce. He wasn't looking for a "good time" girl, he only wanted true love. The kind that lasted a lifetime.

Besides, Daniel was only twenty-nine; he still had many years before he needed to settle down and start a family.

But he knew he could be a bit too outgoing or come off too strong at times. That was something he was working on with the help of his Uncle Steve, the town's veterinarian.

Cody's voice broke through his thoughts. "Do you know her?"

Daniel turned to look at his friend. "No, I don't."

But if Daniel got his way, he would meet her.

<h1 style="text-align:center">Chapter 3</h1>

D aniel hadn't stopped thinking about that pretty cowgirl from the Crooked Arrow Ranch. So when he saw her in town at the Frenchtown Roasting Company, he stopped dead in his tracks and stared. His memory hadn't deceived him—she was just as beautiful as he remembered. To be fair, it had only been a couple of days since Halloween so he shouldn't have worried about his memory.

When the lady turned her gaze on him, she rolled her eyes and looked away. A pang of regret filled his chest. She was just as disgusted with him as he remembered. He'd have to do something to improve her opinion of him.

Daniel wiped his hands on his thighs and headed her way. She was with the same men from the Crooked Arrow as when he'd first seen her on Halloween. They were all standing in line, waiting to place their orders. He got in line directly behind a dark-haired man with a scruffy beard. "Howdy."

The man turned around and grinned. "Hi ya." He looked around the shop. "Isn't it a bit early for Christmas?"

Lottie, the owner of the town's only coffee shop, began decorating right after Halloween. She did a little bit each day, and then on Black Friday it would all come together and her shop looked like a winter wonderland. Last year, Cody had said it looked like Santa's elves threw up all over it. But what else could he expect from the town's grinch?

Daniel grinned and followed the cowboy's gaze. "I take it this is your first year here for Christmas?"

The man nodded. "Yup. I'm Skeeter. Skeeter Murphy." He held his hand out.

Daniel took it. "I'm Daniel Caruthers. Nice to meet you."

Skeeter tapped the man in front of him, who turned around. "Hey Mike, this here is Daniel Caruthers. Daniel, this is Mike Blankenship. He was just gonna tell me why Christmas is already here in the coffee shop but not all along Main Street yet."

With a chuckle, Daniel began to explain how Lottie went all out for Christmas. "This is nothing, just you wait and see how it all looks come the day after Thanksgiving."

Mike didn't say much; he gave more of a wide-eyed grunt. Then it was his turn to place his order.

Daniel noticed that the woman and another man had already placed their orders and moved away. While Mike ordered, Daniel asked Skeeter who the other two were.

"Oh, that's Megan. She's our camp counselor." Skeeter chuckled. "And stay away from Sam, he's an ornery one." Up until that moment, Skeeter seemed like a happy-go-lucky sort of man, but when he spoke about Sam a dark cloud passed over his eyes.

"Is Megan safe with him?" While Daniel didn't understand what Skeeter meant, he hoped that all of the people at the ranch were safe with Sam around. Not that Daniel had had much experience with war veterans, but he had heard plenty of stories about how good men came home so broken that they hurt those they loved. Not on purpose—it was something that happened in war.

"Oh, yes. Jerod, the guy who owns the ranch, wouldn't let anyone stay who wasn't safe to be around. Sam's just…well… let's just say he's a very bitter man."

It was Skeeter's turn to place his order. Daniel had to wait to ask any more questions until after he'd placed his own order. And of course he requested his usual: PSL with a pumpkin scone. Until Lottie stopped selling them, that was all he wanted. Sadly, the coffee shop was very strict about keeping their seasonal items *seasonal*.

"Daniel"—Skeeter stood up and waved to the cowboy —"come join us."

He wasn't about to turn down a chance to talk to the pretty camp counselor, whatever that meant. Daniel picked up his drink and took the plate with his warmed scone and walked over to join them. "Thanks, Skeeter." He sat down and smiled at everyone.

"Megan, Sam, this is Daniel," Skeeter said. "Hey, what is it you do around here?"

"I'm the foreman over at the Christmas tree farm." Daniel took a sip of his pipin'-hot pumpkin spice latte.

Megan gave him a tentative smile. "Nice to meet you."

Sam sneered but said nothing.

"Tough crowd." Daniel held his drink up as he prepared to make a toast. "How about to new friendships?" He quirked a brow, hoping he could get the group to lighten up and at least talk to him. So far, the only one who really wanted to talk was Skeeter.

Daniel was the only one who drank his coffee; the rest stared at him. Although Skeeter did pick up his drink and take a sip after Daniel put his down.

"So…" An awkward pause passed among them all before Daniel continued, "How long have you all been at the Crooked Arrow?"

Skeeter was the first to speak up, and Daniel could tell that he would probably be the only one to welcome Daniel, ever. "I've been here only for a few months."

"Do you like it?" While Daniel hadn't been up to the ranch yet, he had wanted to see what all they were doing. He'd wondered how a ranch could help wounded veterans to heal. It took some serious work to keep a ranch going. Jerod had some cattle along with horses and a few pigs. So far, that was all Daniel had heard about the ranch.

Mike continued to look at the table.

Sam grunted. "What's to like?"

Skeeter, however, seemed genuinely happy. "Hey now, Mike, I know you like the cows. You spend your day either taking care of them, milking them, or making butter and cream. Come on man, tell Daniel here what all you do."

All eyes turned to the quiet man.

Mike looked up at Skeeter, and Daniel noticed an actual feeling cross the big man's face. Was it anger? Or maybe frustration?

"Hey, leave Mike alone. He'll talk when he wants to." Megan glared at Daniel.

Daniel held his hands up. "Hey, I'm good. If Mike wants to share what he likes about living on the ranch, great. If not, I'm still good." He looked to Sam. "How about you? What do you like?"

What Daniel really wanted to know was what Megan liked, but for some reason he couldn't fathom, the woman seemed intent on disliking him.

"I like the peace and quiet when no one else is around." Sam glared at Daniel, then stood up and left the group.

Megan got up to follow the man, but first she too glared at Daniel. "See what you did?"

Totally unsure what had just happened, Daniel looked around as the two men left. "What did I do?"

"Nothing." Mike shook his head. "We should probably go." He stood up and followed the others outside.

Skeeter put a hand on Daniel's shoulder. "Hey man, don't worry. Sam's what we call 'socially challenged.' And for some reason Megan thinks it's her job to protect him. Catch you around." Then he stood up with his coffee in one hand and tried to maneuver his way out of the coffee shop on his crutches.

"Hey, let me help." Daniel stood up and took the coffee cup from Skeeter.

Once they were outside, Mike took the cup and gave Daniel a small half-smile.

Skeeter, oblivious as to who had his coffee cup, thanked Daniel.

When Daniel went back inside to his latte, he sat down hard. "Well, that's a first."

Chapter 4

"**M**en are so infuriating." Megan slammed her fist down on the kitchen table at the Crooked Arrow Ranch.

Jerod Stevens held up his hands while standing in the doorway. "Whoa now. Who's infuriating? All men, or one in particular?" His eyes sparkled and he grinned at Megan.

"Ugh, happily engaged men are even worse." Megan stood up and took her coffee mug to the kitchen sink.

"Hey, Megan. I can't have my one and only counselor upset. Come on, tell me what's wrong." Jerod took a seat at the table and patted the chair she had just vacated.

She sighed and leaned against the kitchen counter. "It's not you or anyone here. Don't worry. It was just my first chance to express my frustration about a man we met in town earlier, that's all." She waved off Jerod's concern.

She really wasn't worried about the guy. And if she was being honest with herself, the Prince Harry lookalike wasn't that bad. He just seemed to think he was God's gift, and that was all that bugged her. She hated it when men knew they were good-looking, and Daniel most certainly knew it.

The way he'd smiled and winked at her, it was though he thought he was being nice by paying her attention. She didn't even need his attention, nor want it. Not after she saw how conceited he was. She'd had her share of men who thought they were all that and a bag of candy canes. Nope, she was done with self-absorbed men.

Jerod put his hand over his mouth and tried to cover a smile. "Does this have anything to do with the ginger-haired cowboy you met in town today?"

Megan's head jerked back in surprise. "How did you hear… Never mind. Skeeter can't keep his mouth shut."

"Actually, it was Mike."

"What? Mike told you something that had nothing to do with cows? Did you sit him down and interrogate him?" Megan chortled. Even though Jerod had been special forces, she knew he'd never interrogate any of his guests or employees. And certainly not over some egotistical cowboy.

"I think you know better." Jerod chuckled. "No, Mike wanted to talk to me about it. He was confused about your attitude."

Her eyes bulged, and Megan put a hand on her chest. "My attitude? I wasn't the one who thought he was too good for the rest of us."

Jerod sat there for a moment, then tilted his head. "This guy's gotten under your skin, hasn't he? Does he remind you of someone?"

"Pft." Megan's shoulders jumped when she scoffed. "Just about every other man who thinks he's God's gift."

"So, he's good-looking?"

"Ugh, get over it, will ya?" Megan moved to leave the kitchen. She'd had enough of this talk. And besides, who was the one with a master's degree in psychology and the treatment of PTSD? Oh, that's right—it was her. Not Jerod.

Jerod's deep chuckle followed her out of the kitchen and all the way up the stairs to her office. When she shut the door, the noise finally died. "Who cares if he's good-looking? What does that have to do with anything?"

"Who's good-looking? Me?" Skeeter Murphy was sitting in the chair across from her desk.

Megan jumped and put a hand to her chest. After she let out a breath, she looked at her wristwatch; she was two minutes late for their afternoon session. "Sorry, Skeeter. I got help up downstairs. How are you doing today? I mean really?"

They spent the next fifty minutes talking about how Skeeter was acclimating to civilian life, and his last nightmare. They were getting fewer and far between. Megan was sure that once his physical ailments healed he'd be in good shape mentally, and he'd be ready to leave the ranch. But she wasn't sure if she wanted the easygoing vet to leave. He was her best patient.

Okay, sure, he was a bit too friendly with everyone in town, but there wasn't anything wrong with being outgoing. It would serve him well once he went looking for a civilian job. Maybe he'd even end up on a ranch.

Thinking about her patients was so much easier than thinking about that…that…Daniel Caruthers. She'd even prefer to think about Sam Marley over the ginger-haired cowboy.

Chapter 5

When Daniel woke up, he had no clue how much snow would be on the ground. It was good and bad. The worst part was that he was going to have to help Cody clean the walkways around the farm. He lived in town with his uncle, the town's veterinarian, so he still had to drive out to the tree farm. Thankfully the plows had just gone through town and cleared those streets.

Unfortunately they hadn't cleared the road leading to the tree farm, so it was slow going on the way to work. "If only I'd gone into the Frenchtown Roasting Company for a PSL...and a scrumptious pumpkin scone." Daniel was dreaming of the sweet and spicy drizzle that coated the fluffy scone when he heard a noise behind him.

"Of course. My timing is always perfect." Even though he was talking to himself, he recognized the sarcasm in his voice. From the rearview mirror he could see the snowplow behind him. The sad part was that it was driving faster than he was.

Daniel had two choices: speed up and take a chance on spinning out, or pull over to the left side of the road and let the plow pass him, hoping no cars would come at him from the opposite direction. If he chose the latter he'd have a nice, clean ride as far as the plow went. It should go past the tree farm before turning around. Or at least he hoped it would.

"Oh, son of a fruitcake!" Daniel pounded the steering wheel when he remembered that he was supposed to call the city maintenance department and inform them that the tree lot was opening early and would need the plows to keep the roads clear for the rest of the year.

He made a quick decision to pull to the left to allow the machine to pass him. Then he'd follow the plow just to see how far out it went. If it wasn't so early, he'd call the maintenance department while he was waiting and make sure they knew of the change in dates. They had a standing order with the city and county to ensure that the roads in and out of the tree farm were clear from the middle of November all the way through Christmas.

However, since they'd made a last-minute change in schedule this year and decided to open three weeks early, it was on him to notify everyone. But with all of the extra work the past few weeks and the calendar shoot, well, not everything had been done on time.

The one bright spot on that cold, gray day was that someone had already informed the maintenance crew about the change in plans. As Daniel followed the plow into work, he noticed that another one was already working in front of the farm clearing the other side of the road, as well as their small makeshift parking lot—a bare piece of land used for overflow parking. That would make things much easier for him. Maybe it would be a good day after all.

Famous last words.

Not two hours later the place was busier than they'd ever seen before Black Friday, and the news report hadn't even aired yet. They weren't coming until next weekend, when they had the calendars.

"Is this what social media can do to a business?" Daniel stood next to Cody watching the craziness of the people parking all willy nilly and mothers trying to keep ahold of their kids. It was his job to do the sleigh rides that day; he'd already taken out six families, and more were lined up. He'd only taken a break to get more hot coffee. With lines like this he'd need a second sleigh, and another driver.

Since there was a coffee line, Daniel headed to the barn where they had a coffee pot going all day long just for the employees. Cody followed him, which didn't surprise Daniel when he noticed Sadie standing there talking to the group from the Crooked Arrow Ranch. But what did surprise him were the bees buzzing around in his belly when he looked at Megan.

She sure was a pretty sight. The lovely counselor wore a red puffy coat with white faux-fur trim around the edges. Her red snow boots matched the coat perfectly. She reminded him of a model in one of those winter clothes catalogs. He knew she hadn't noticed him yet because her smile was genuine and sweet.

Sadly, her sweet smile turned sour when she did get a look at him. But Daniel wasn't going to let her get to him. No siree, Frosty. He was going to find a way to get Megan to like him.

That thought stopped him short. Why did he care so much if the little cowgirl liked him or not?

When Megan scowled at his smile, he decided to play with her a little. "Why Megan, I'm just as happy to see you as you are to see me." Daniel winked at her, and he knew he had gotten to her when he noticed her shiver. If he wasn't mistaken, she was *trying* to *not* like him. That was it. Eventually she'd give up the fight.

Before Megan could respond to his teasing, Santa and Mrs. Claus joined them. Daniel always loved it when the Clauses were around. They brought a little extra Christmas magic with them wherever they went, especially when they were all dressed up in their Santa gear, as they were at that moment. Having the most popular couple from the North Pole join them every year at Christmas only helped their sales. But that wasn't why Daniel loved having them around.

Since Daniel didn't have much family, he didn't have a big Christmas Day celebration. It was usually just him and his Uncle Steve. Sometimes his mother would come visit, but it had been years since she'd come to town. She was married to Ray Seward, a rancher from South Dakota, so traveling wasn't as easy for her. And Daniel couldn't leave the farm until Christmas Day. So it never made much sense to him to head out to his mom's place. Besides, if he left then Uncle Steve would be all alone.

His uncle had helped to raise him, and he never wanted to let him be alone. Usually the two of them would head out to Cody's house for Christmas dinner with Cody and his grandpops. The four of them would have a meal fit for a king, or four kings in their case, and watch football games on TV.

But when Santa was around, he'd remember what it was like as a kid and the excitement would come back. Daniel enjoyed helping other kids have a good Christmas. Every year he secretly worked with Santa to ensure that disadvantaged kids around the area got what they wanted and needed. He wasn't the only one, but most of Santa's Helpers stayed anonymous, like him.

He also enjoyed sleigh rides.

"Well, I best be going. The line for the sleigh rides is getting kinda long." Daniel waved to the group and then looked directly at Megan. "You know, the farm is pretty spectacular when viewed from a sleigh. You might consider taking a ride one of these days." He winked again, only because he knew it got under her skin and he loved to get a reaction from her. It told him she had some feelings toward him. He wasn't sure if she was interested yet, but at least she wasn't totally immune to his charm.

Chapter 6

M egan couldn't believe the gall of that cowboy. *How could anyone be so confident in his charm?* No, she wasn't going to think of him. And she certainly wasn't going on a sleigh ride with him. Although, the idea of a sleigh ride through the snowy Christmas tree farm did sound wonderful. While she'd never been on one, she sure had seen plenty of Christmas romance movies where an evening sleigh ride through snow and lights seemed very romantic.

In fact, in her favorite Christmas movie the starring couple rode through a beautiful forest with the trees covered in lights while snow fell lightly on the ground. The boyfriend proposed to his lady love, and they lived happily ever after. She knew it was just a movie, but it sure was romantic. In real life, romance and chivalry were dead.

Okay, okay, maybe not dead. But in her experience, Megan had yet to meet a gentleman who knew how to woo a lady. Most of the men she'd gone out with were all hands and had just one thing on their mind—not in this lifetime. Hades would have to freeze over and become the winter wonderland that the Big Sky Christmas Tree Farm had become before she'd succumb to any of the players she'd dated. Which was why she had stopped dating.

It was hopeless.

Men were hopeless.

Honestly, Megan knew there were good guys out there. One of her high school girlfriends had married one and they were very happy living in Florida with their white picket fence, two point five kids, and a dog.

Not that Megan really wanted that particular dream, but she did want to get married and have kids. But not to just anyone. With her background, she knew she'd never marry anyone unless she was absolutely certain he was *the one*. And so far, it was only *the one for tonight* kind of guys who asked her out.

Besides, with Megan's military background, she doubted anyone but a soldier would do for her. She might consider an airman, but certainly no Marines or sailors for her. Well, unless he was a frogman. It had been a joke with her Army pals; they always made fun of the other branches of service. She also knew that the other branches made fun of the Army. But the main reason she didn't think she'd end up with a civvie was because most civilians just didn't understand what it was like to serve. Especially when a veteran had been involved with war.

Even her patients at the ranch had a hard time explaining what they'd gone through while deployed. While she'd never come across any of them during her time in Afghanistan, she had been there at the same time as some of these guys and she understood what they were trying to say. But more importantly, she understood how it felt to be under attack. Modern warfare was nothing like what she had learned about in history. Fighting in the Middle East wasn't standard warfare. The rules of engagement were different than anything she had ever read about.

But she didn't want to think about what she had seen while in country. No, she was ready to put it all behind her and look to the future. A future that didn't include cocky cowboys who had never put on a uniform. And she couldn't ethically date her patients, so she'd probably end up a spinster, which was just fine with her.

That was until she realized she was watching said cowboy help an elderly lady and her husband get into the sleigh for a ride. Daniel was gentle and congenial with them. He didn't flirt with the woman or even wink at her. At least, not that Megan could tell from where she stood. But he did smile at the couple and waved at the crowd of people lined up for their turn on the sleigh.

"He's kinda cute, isn't he?" Sadie stood next to Megan, watching with her.

Megan startled. She had been so in her own head that she hadn't realized anyone had walked up to her. "What? Who?" She looked away from Daniel, her cheeks warming up.

"Daniel really is a nice guy. I don't know what's going with you two, but give him a chance." Sadie walked away before Megan could deny there was anything going on. Shoot, she'd barely met the guy, how could there be anything going on?

Sure, he resembled a ruggedly handsome prince, but that didn't mean she was into him. Megan would bet any woman with eyes would think he was nice-looking. In fact, Sadie had just said so. Which was probably why he was so cocky. That was a trait that turned her off.

Or was he only cocky with her? Megan turned her eyes back to the man as he led the sleigh with the elderly couple through the trees.

Maybe she should take a ride on the sleigh. It wouldn't hurt to at least check out the trees; the ranch was going to need at least two of them. And if Jerod was a typical guy, he'd forget to pick out a tree until it was too late. Although, his fiance would probably help him. There was a great idea: Megan should reach out to Dana and see if she wanted to help her pick out trees.

They could even take the sleigh ride together to see what all was still available.

Megan and Dana had become fast friends. Dana Baker, who worked at the Frenchtown Roasting Company, had met and begun dating Jerod Stevens only a few months ago, right before Megan came to the ranch. While they didn't know each other that well, Megan did like the young woman a lot. She seemed to have her head on straight, and from what the gossip mill at the ranch had said, she really helped to ground Jerod.

Dana and Jerod were getting married in the spring, and Megan couldn't be happier to have another woman on the ranch. So far, all of the patients that came to the ranch were men. She knew there would eventually be women who needed their services as well, but it just hadn't happened yet. And being the only woman on a ranch full of men wasn't all fun and games.

One thing she'd learned quickly was that cowboys gossip just as much as the little old church ladies. Those guys were a hoot. Or maybe it was just cowboys who had once been in the military? She couldn't be sure since she really only knew the guys on her ranch. And all of them had been in the military at one time or another, including the ones who only worked there and weren't her patients.

Megan pulled out her cell phone and dialed Dana. Once she was done making her plans, she went and found the guys to take them back to the ranch. They were only supposed to be at the Christmas tree farm for a short visit to check the place out. But before she found the guys, she found Sadie. "Hey, there. Looks like y'all are gonna have a bumper season. I don't know how you're gonna handle all of these people."

Sadie frowned and ran a hand down her face. "I know. I'm wondering the same thing." She looked around. "But do me a favor and don't say anything to Cody or Daniel. I need to figure this out, and quickly. Something tells me that next weekend is gonna be a madhouse, one I'm not quite prepared for."

"Don't worry." Megan grinned. "Mum's the word."

"Thanks."

While Megan wrangled her charges, she thought about how they could help the tree farm. One of the things that Megan had learned while getting her degree was how much giving back helped those who had problems of their own. While some of her clients out at the ranch wouldn't do well interacting with the public, others like Skeeter would do really well.

Speak of the devil. Megan watched as Skeeter flirted with a blushing young woman. She shook her head and decided to go save the girl. She couldn't have been more than eighteen or nineteen and probably not used to such attention, although she was a pretty girl.

"Skeeter, are you being nice?" Megan put her hands on her hips and stared him down.

The man in question rested on one crutch while the other was leaned up against the wall of a craft shop. "Why, of course I am. I'm always nice." He winked at the young girl, who blushed even deeper and looked to the ground.

Megan felt for the girl. Skeeter was harmless, but he could be a handful. "Miss, don't mind my friend here." She pointed to the cowboy. "He's usually a nice guy, but sometimes he can be a handful."

"Ouch." Skeeter put a hand over his chest. "That hurt."

A chortle escaped Megan's lips. "Yeah, right. Anyway, if you want a ride back, I'm leaving now." She wanted to say more to the girl, but decided she'd leave Skeeter to his own devices. The girl was probably too young for Skeeter anyway.

"Annabeth, I'll be back next weekend if you're out this way again." The look on Skeeter's face was something she hadn't seen coming from him before. He seemed more serious and subdued than normal. Megan wondered if he'd known this Annabeth before today or if there was some sort of connection there.

"Okay, if my parents will let me use the truck, I'll come back on Saturday afternoon." Annabeth looked up through her long black eyelashes and gave Skeeter a sweet smile before waving goodbye.

Once Annabeth was out of earshot, Megan grinned from ear to ear. "So, you've got yourself a girlfriend?" She shoved his shoulder just a bit, careful not to knock him over.

Skeeter still wasn't steady on his feet, and he'd need the crutches for a few more months before he could start using a cane. The doctor had offered him the use of a walker, but the manly cowboy said walkers were for old coots, and he wasn't old. Besides, it was only temporary.

"Nah, she's a sweet girl, barely out of high school." His cheeks began to pink, something that Megan thought she'd never see on this guy.

"So then why are you meeting her here next week?"

Skeeter shrugged. "I don't know. Bored, I guess."

Megan knew better. He liked the girl. She was a bit young for him; Skeeter was twenty-five years old, though he was a bit immature. So maybe an eighteen-year-old would be about right for him. As long as he was a perfect gentleman, she'd leave him be.

Although, she couldn't guarantee Sam wouldn't harass him if he saw anything.

She took Skeeter and found the other guys and headed back to their ranch. The guys had chores to do, and Megan needed to be sure to get them home in time.

It had been a good outing. The men seemed to do well, and even Mike had a smile on his face as they all loaded into the pickup.

"Mike, did you have fun?" Megan looked at him through her rearview mirror before pulling out on the road home.

With a smile still etched on his face, Mike nodded. "I liked the craft booths. One of the women said she crocheted when she was stressed out and it helped. She had a lot of different items, including a few afghans for sale."

Sam scoffed. "Crocheting is for old ladies, not men."

"Hey, all crafting is for anyone who wants to do it. In fact, when I was in school we had a special class dedicated to the health benefits of crafting." Megan had thought about starting up a crafting group at the ranch, but she wasn't really all that great with sewing or crocheting. She might have to speak with some of the women who had the booths and see if they could come out and do a demonstration some time.

"I like woodworking," Skeeter volunteered. "My dad used to have his own shop and I'd go help out after school sometimes."

"Really? There's an idea. But we don't have any power saws, jigs, or whatever it is you need to do woodworking." Megan bit her lip. It would cost a lot of money to get some of these tools for the patients to work on, and they didn't have much of the grant money left.

"You don't always need expensive tools. I've got some hand tools that my mom sent me. I use them for whittling." In fact, Skeeter had been seen around the farm carving small pieces of wood when he had free time. And usually he whistled while he whittled.

Skeeter was in the front seat, so Megan only turned her head slightly to look at the man. "Do you think you could show some of the other men how to do it?"

He shrugged. "Sure, if anyone wants to learn I can teach them. It's easy. And you don't even need working legs to do it, just hands."

Before Skeeter realized what he had said, Sam growled from the back seat. "I don't got two hands."

Megan felt for Sam. Ever since losing his left arm, he'd felt as though he wasn't fully a man. Which only baffled Megan. His prosthetic arm was fairly decent as long as he wore a long-sleeve shirt and gloves. She knew he could do just about anything anyone else could do. Sure, Sam wouldn't ever be a professional drawer, at least not with his left hand. But wasn't the man right-handed? He could do everything he did before with his right hand.

"Sam, your right hand is just fine. And your left hand works very well. If you focused, you could learn how to hold the piece of wood in your left hand and use the tools in your right." She had learned long ago that speaking in a soft, soothing voice usually calmed the beast within the angry men. And Sam most definitely fell into that category.

Skeeter wasn't angry, but he could be a little short-sighted at times. He turned around and looked at Sam sitting in the back seat. "I'm sorry, man. I didn't mean anything by it. You so could learn to whittle. Like Megan said"—he pointed to the driver —"you really only need your right hand to do anything. The left holds it."

Sam didn't respond. Instead he looked out the window, still angry at the world.

Since coming to the Crooked Arrow Ranch, Sam was the only one who had shown very little improvement in his attitude and how he viewed himself. Megan and Jerod both wondered if Sam would ever be able to integrate fully back into society. Before coming to the ranch, he had been in an alcohol detox program. No alcohol or drugs of any sort were allowed at the ranch. If anyone was caught drinking or taking drugs, even prescription drugs outside of the way they were prescribed, they'd be kicked out.

Megan prayed that Sam wouldn't spiral and get back into old habits. Too many returning veterans numbed their pain with drugs or alcohol. Part of her training was in spotting when someone was doing something illicit, or about to get themselves into trouble. Since she'd arrived, she had worried about Sam. He had seemed on the edge of a cliff every day.

After they returned, Megan pulled Jerod aside. "I'm worried about Sam. Something innocuous was said today and he really took it hard. He needs something to help him feel as though he's contributing to society without actually being out there for all the world to see his arm."

"Funny you should say that," Jerod said. "I just got off the phone with Sadie. She said they could use some more help over at the tree farm next weekend. Maybe you can take a couple of the guys, including Sam, and see what they need next Saturday? Sadie was confident that they'd have no issues tomorrow, but with the news showcasing them next weekend it'll most likely get crazy over there." Jerod could always be counted on to come up with good ideas to help the guys.

Even though Megan was the one with the degree, Jerod was the one with ranch experience. And thanks to his own issues recovering from an attack, he knew enough that he could always be counted on. "Thanks, I'll get Sam and see if anyone else wants to head back next Saturday to help out."

Jerod's statement about the farm needing help the following weekend seemed more like a premonition than anything else.

Chapter 7

It was too soon for them to pick out a Christmas tree. It wasn't even close to Thanksgiving yet; November had barely started. But the tree lot was open for the second weekend this month, with mini-barns that Daniel and Cody had made for the crafters and other artisans to sell their wares for Christmas.

This year was much different than any Daniel had worked before. Normally they opened a few days before Thanksgiving and only sold trees and wreaths. This year, Cody had come up with several ideas to make enough money to save the tree farm, and his job. Daniel would do anything he could to help his friend save the farm that his family had started, and in the process save his own job.

So they were open to the public now, and thanks to some exciting social media posts the tree farm had customers coming to their mini-carnival and Christmas fair. Not to mention the fact that they were doing tree pre-sales for the first time ever.

The mini-carnival had set up to the side of the farm's main barn, on the other side of the craft fair area. They had brought in kiddie rides and a few game booths. This weekend they also had a hot dog truck. Thanks to the traffic from last weekend, Cody knew it would be even bigger this weekend.

He and Cody had worked during the week to make a few more of the mini-barn booths, and the local diner had even come in with pots of beef stew and soup—which Daniel was very grateful for.

Maybe that was what the pretty girl from the Crooked Arrow was here for, too? The diner made a fantastic beef stew, but Daniel preferred their clam chowder with freshly made sourdough rolls. In fact, he was already salivating over what he would eat for lunch, and that was still two hours away.

Megan had come to the farm the previous weekend and she had seen most everything. Maybe she was here to see the new booths? Or was it possible she wanted to see him? He doubted it, but the thought did put a smile on his face.

Deciding he didn't want to wait any longer to find out what Megan was there for, Daniel headed her way with a big, welcoming grin on his face. Unlike his boss, Daniel almost always had a smile for people. Shoot, he even smiled for the animals when no one else was around.

"Hi, welcome to the Big Sky Christmas Tree Farm." Daniel waved at the group and held his hand out to Megan. "It's nice to see you again. And I see you've brought a couple of new guys." He looked at the two men whom he hadn't met yet.

The new guys waved, but only Skeeter smiled. Sam looked as though he'd eaten something bad. And Mike didn't look him in the eye; instead he looked down at his boots.

"Hi Daniel." Megan didn't look too happy to see him, but she wasn't turning her back on him, so that was progress, wasn't it?

"What can I help you with today?" Daniel wasn't going to let a couple of grumps get him down. He was used to it anyway, with Cody being the town's grinch and all.

"Well, Jerod thought we could come out here and help." Megan bit her lower lip and looked around at the forming crowds. "It seems you have more customers than you realized."

Daniel frowned. "What do you mean?"

"What she means," Sam interrupted with a gravelly voice, "is that you've got lines of people all over the place. If you aren't careful, someone's gonna get hurt."

Daniel rubbed the back of his neck. They did need people to help with crowd control, but he knew Cody couldn't afford to pay anyone.

Sadie walked up to the group before Daniel could say anything and he let out a sigh of relief. "Megan, it's good to see you again. Welcome to the farm." Sadie reached out to hug the woman.

Daniel didn't realize the two of them had become friends. He'd have to ask Sadie what she knew about the pretty lady. And also see if she could put in a good word for him. But first, he needed to know what to do about the people offering to help.

"Sadie, Jerod and I were wondering if there was anything we could do to help this weekend? And these here guys"—she pointed to the men next to her—"would like to help."

Daniel still didn't know who two of them were, but Sadie seemed to. "Arthur and Dixon, welcome to the farm. Is this your first time here?"

Arthur nodded, and Dixon answered in the affirmative before turning his wide eyes to the loud people all around. The young man winced when a kid ran by yelling about how excited he was to be there.

While Arthur was quiet, he didn't seem to mind all the noise. The man seemed relaxed and in his element.

But Dixon seemed to be in over his head. The young man couldn't have been older than twenty-one or twenty-two. And when he walked Daniel noticed he moved strangely, almost like he was injured. Then Daniel realized the guy had come from the Crooked Arrow. Dixon was probably there to recuperate after taking shrapnel to his leg, or something like that.

"Sorry, where are my manners?" The pink that tinged Megan's cheeks sent a thrill up Daniel's back. "Sadie, Daniel, this is Arthur and Dixon." Megan pointed to the two men in turn. "And you both know Sam, Skeeter, and Mike, right?"

"Yes, good to see you guys again. Arthur and Dixon, I hope you enjoy your time here today." Daniel shook hands with all the men and looked at Megan with his brows raised. He wanted to shake her hand, but she never seemed very receptive to him.

So when she put her hand out, he had to work to keep his jaw from hitting the ground. Then when he took her hand, all restraint left him and he took a step closer and covered her hand with his free one.

A warmth flowed through his hands and up his arms as he touched her. It felt familiar, yet new.

Megan furrowed her brow and broke the touch. But Daniel noticed her wide eyes and how warm her hands were. So when pink covered her cheeks again, he knew she'd felt the instant connection just as much as he had.

She cleared her throat and looked to Sadie. "I was wondering if you could use any help today? A few of our guys wanted to come and check the place out and maybe lend a hand. It isn't every day one gets to see the inner workings of a Christmas tree farm."

Sadie grinned. "We could use a few volunteers to guide people in to the lot from the road. And maybe a few to help with picking out trees." She looked to the guys. "Do any of you know about Christmas trees?"

Skeeter put his hands on his belt. "Yup."

Arthur nodded.

The rest all shook their heads.

Daniel grinned at Megan. "I could always use help from a pretty gal."

Megan cringed, and the men from her ranch all stepped in closer to her.

Daniel knew he'd messed up. While he may flirt a lot, he wasn't great at talking to women. His uncle had diagnosed him with "foot-in-mouth disease" when he was a teenager and got his face slapped for saying something that came out all wrong. He hadn't intended to make the girl feel bad about herself, he just got tongue-tied when it was a really pretty girl that he might be interested in.

Which made him think back to the previous conversations he'd had with Megan. As far as he could tell, he hadn't said anything too bad. But maybe he had without realizing it and that was why she never seemed to like him.

The smile on Sadie's face was fake, and Daniel knew it. Yup, he'd really messed up. Maybe there was more to it?

"I've got this, Daniel. Why don't you go back to running the sleigh rides?" Just like that, Sadie dismissed him.

He started to walk away and then realized he could use help. Real help, from one of the guys. "Hey, do any of you know how to drive a sleigh?"

The Crooked Arrow Ranch guys glared at him before relaxing their faces and looking at each other. Then Mike raised a hand. "I've driven sleighs several times before I joined the Army."

Well, that was a surprise. Daniel had barely heard this man talk, and now he was volunteering to help with the sleigh. He tilted his head and thought about the quiet man. It didn't take much talking to run the sleigh. Most people didn't ask questions, they just looked out at the scenery and spoke among themselves. "Great. I can take you out and show you the route if you'd like?"

For the first time ever, Daniel watched as Mike's face lit up. Maybe this guy was a rancher at heart?

"Yeah, that'd be great." Mike turned to Megan. "Is that alright?"

Megan blinked a few times and nodded. "Yeah… I mean if you want, sure."

To make sure he didn't do or say anything wrong again, Daniel waved at the group and motioned for Mike Blankenship to follow him. That morning one of the other guys they had hired for the season was running the sleigh. So when it came back in Daniel introduced the two men, and Javier—the one who was running the sleigh rides that morning—helped Mike learn the ropes.

Daniel grinned and watched the two men take a family out on the sleigh. He knew Mike was shy and never really came out of his shell. Well, unless he was with the cows. Or at least, that's what Megan said. So to see him excited about running the sleigh felt good. When they did more hiring, he'd have to talk to Cody about hiring more of the Crooked Arrow Ranch guys. Maybe some of these guys just needed a chance to help others in a safe environment. One thing he knew for sure: Cody would want to help them if he could.

The only problem was cash flow. But as he turned around and saw all of the people there spending money, Daniel knew cash flow wouldn't be an issue for too much longer.

When lunchtime rolled around, Daniel's stomach was gurgling up a storm. He really needed to eat more for breakfast on days when the farm was open. He never seemed to stop moving. Even though he was eating a late lunch, the line was longer than he had hoped. Even managing the farm didn't earn him the right to cut the line.

But knowing someone who was up close might help.

"Thanks for saving me a spot." Daniel walked up to the pretty woman in a red parka and red snow boots that he'd recognize anywhere—Megan.

"Oh, it's you. Actually, I was saving a spot for a gentleman friend of mine." The smirk on Megan's face was priceless.

Daniel knew without a shadow of a doubt that this woman enjoyed their banter. "Oh, really? And would that gentleman happen to be the foreman of this here tree farm?" He arched a brow and took two steps forward with her when the line moved.

Megan looked around. "Actually, I hear the foreman is a bit rude and thinks he's better than anyone else."

Did she really think that of him? Or was it just part of the game they were playing? "Hmm, maybe it's just a defensive wall he's got up?"

She opened her mouth and then shut it. It was a moment before Megan said anything again. "But why?"

Daniel shrugged. "Sometimes men hide behind a persona just like women do."

It was their turn to order. Daniel let Megan order first, then he placed his order for the clam chowder. When he handed his credit card to the cashier, Megan put her hand up.

"I can pay for my own, thank you."

He pursed his lips. "I may not be the gentleman you were expecting, but I was raised to treat women right."

"Is that so?" Megan almost laughed.

The cashier let him pay for both of their meals and asked them to move to the side to continue their argument.

"Argument? I didn't think we were arguing. Did you?" Daniel wasn't sure what the cashier was thinking, but he hoped Megan didn't agree with her.

Megan's nose scrunched up and she shook her head. "No, I thought we were discussing who was going to pay… Hey, she didn't take my card. Did you pay?"

"Now that this is an official date, do I get a kiss at the end?" Daniel laughed and moved away when she tried to slap his shoulder. Not that it would have hurt; he had on his thick Carhartt jacket that did more than just keep out the cold—it also kept women from leaving a sting on his shoulder.

"Grrr." Megan threw up her hands. "I knew I shouldn't have come to lunch alone." She turned to walk away.

"Megan, wait. I'm sorry. I was just teasing. Probably not the right thing to say to someone who doesn't like me."

She narrowed her eyes at him. "Do you know how to be honest? Or serious? All you do is joke and make stupid comments."

Daniel rubbed the back of his neck, but before he could respond their number was called and Megan went to get her bowl of beef stew.

"Okay, so this isn't a date. But would you still like to sit and share your lunch with me? I know a warm place we can sit and eat that's out of the way." The least he could do was offer her a spot at their lunch table in the barn. People wouldn't be all over the place and they could talk.

"Out of the way? What, like in your room?" She pursed her lips and shook her head before walking away from him.

"What? I didn't say that. And I wasn't even thinking that. Honest," Daniel called out as he followed her.

Megan turned around. "Look, thanks for lunch, but I don't think I can stomach any more of your stimulating conversation." Then she turned and went to join Sam at a table. It was under a tarp, so snow wouldn't get on them, but it was far from warm.

Under his breath, Daniel objected again. "But I was just going to bring you to the employee lunch area in the barn. We have a space heater there." Feeling dejected, he walked by himself and ate his lunch all alone.

But Daniel didn't have much time to think about Megan again that afternoon. Cody needed his help and they were busy all afternoon. When it was getting close to time for the weather girl to show up and do her report, Daniel went to see where they were going to set up.

Then a loud bang sounded and people started screaming and yelling. A few ran toward the exit. All of the lights went out and it was almost pitch black. The calmer people pulled out their cell phones and activated their flashlight app. It provided enough light for Daniel to make his way to the barn and grab a flashlight. He'd need to help calm people down while Cody worked on getting the lights back on.

The moment he turned on his flashlight, Cody showed up and pulled him to the back of the barn. "We've gotta get these lights on."

"Do you know what happened?" Daniel hadn't seen them lose power ever, so this was a shock to him. Then again, they usually had a temporary power line already set up with more power than they needed before they opened. This year, since they'd made the changes at the last minute, they couldn't get the power line installed early.

"I should have known we'd blow a fuse." Cody pulled out the main circuit breaker and watched as it smoked. "Well, I guess that's more than a blown fuse."

"Can you fix it?" Daniel asked.

"Yeah, it's going to take a few minutes. In the meantime, can you get the emergency generators turned on?"

Chapter 8

The moment Megan heard the explosion, she watched Arthur run for the barn. At first she was afraid the sound was too much for him. Then she realized that Cody and Daniel were over there already and knew what Arthur was doing.

Arthur Landsbury had been an electrical engineer in the Army, so of course when the power went out he ran to the noise to see if he could help.

Megan felt herself sigh in relief when she realized he wasn't freaking out. But there were other men with her who suffered from PTSD, and she had to find them right away. She pulled her phone out and looked to see if there were any messages—none. Then she turned on her flashlight app and searched around.

Eventually she spotted Dixon rolled up like a kitten on his side near the front gate. She ran to him and whispered in a soothing voice, "Shh, everything's alright. I'm here now. Shhh." She ran a hand over his head and he tightened even further into a little ball. "Dixon, it was just the power going out at the Christmas tree farm. You're safe. You have nothing to fear."

She sat down next to him and continued to run her hand over his head. The poor man's forehead was covered in sweat. But as she continued to console him, she felt his body slowly relax.

Bringing Dixon had been a mistake. The kid was in pretty good shape, all things considered, but he wasn't ready for crowds. As she continued to console him, she looked around at the people, hoping to see at least one of her guys.

After what felt like hours, but must have only been ten minutes, the lights came back on and the people around Megan started to calm down. She looked to the mini-midway and saw that the carnival lights were also coming back online. It didn't surprise her that the carnival had generators; she'd seen the large power supplies on wheels behind their carts and rides. It would be loud having them operate on their generators, but it would also be worth it to make sure the show went on.

And the show did go on, much to Megan's surprise.

The rest of her guys found her and Dixon—well, except for Arthur, whom she'd seen running to help Daniel and Cody. But standing next to her now, watching the weather girl give her meteorological report, were Dixon, Sam, and Skeeter. She had to assume Mike was still working the sleigh rides. Skeeter assured her that the sound wouldn't have bothered Mike, especially if he was out on the sleigh. They had battery operated lanterns on the sleigh. And since the power came back on so quickly, the lights which had been strung all over the trees would help to guide Mike back into the farm. Probably one of the reasons the circuit breaker popped like it did was all of those extra lights.

Megan had to admit, it was a loud sound and even she had jerked and looked around when the loud boom went off. But now everyone seemed alright, and most of the lights had been restored. Plus, the light coming from the news crew was enough to make it almost look like daytime. As soon as she could get Arthur and Mike, Megan would be taking the guys home and ensuring that they had a group session that night for all who needed it. And Dixon would get a one-on-one session as soon as he felt up to it.

But when she suggested they leave, all of the men, Dixon included, said they wanted to stay for the rest of the evening. They weren't about to give up, or give in to their fears. They were soldiers and Marines.

"We left the zoomies back at the ranch. None of us are afraid." Sam stood taller and smirked at Megan.

Zoomies were what most service members called the Air Force. It was a bit on the derogatory side, but all branches had similar nicknames for each other. It was all done in jest. If anyone actually threatened an airman, then a soldier, or even a Marine, would totally stand up for them.

Something about serving one's country produced a bond that went across all branches, even though they loved to tease one another.

"So, a pretty crazy day, right?" Megan asked as they headed back toward the truck after the place closed.

"Hey boss, I offered to help Daniel and Cody on Tuesday when the power company brings their temporary line out. Is that alright?" Arthur had been in high spirits when he joined them after the news report was concluded and the temporary fix for the power was all set up.

In fact, all but Dixon and Sam seemed fine. To be fair, Sam was always in a mood, so she couldn't be sure if the power outage had affected him or not. Since it was Megan's job to ensure their physical well-being as well as their mental, she would have to have a chat with Sam, too.

"Tuesday? You wanna come back when they're closed?" Megan sighed. She knew she'd have to be the one to bring Arthur back. But this was a good thing. While the man had been helpful on the ranch, this was the first time he had asked to do something helpful. In the past he never complained when given an assignment, but he'd never shown much interest in the running of the ranch. Maybe it was just because the chores weren't exactly exciting. I mean, who enjoyed mucking out stalls?

"Yes, ma'am."

Megan nodded. "Alright, let me talk with Jerod to ensure that he doesn't already have plans for you. If he says it's alright, you can come back to help."

Each of the patients had to do so many hours a month in community service. Not because they were being punished, but because this was one way to help the returning veterans get back into civilian life. Giving back was also a great way to help them clear their minds and focus on something, or someone, other than themselves and their issues.

Frenchtown had a lot of community events coming up, and most of the men had offered to help with setup and teardown for the various events. It was something the town needed, and it was also physical enough to help the men to feel better about their own disabilities. But offering something else would be a great alternative for those who weren't quite ready to do lifting and carrying. Maybe something at the tree farm could be offered to those who didn't spook easily and weren't quite ready to lift anything heavy yet?

The work her guys did at the tree farm that weekend was volunteer, and went toward their weekly quota of hours. But there were other men at the Crooked Arrow who needed something to do as well.

With all of these thoughts in mind, the time went quickly and Jerod was waiting for them when Megan pulled into the driveway.

"Hey, how'd it go? I watched the news report." Jerod eyed the men, and his gaze stayed on Dixon a few heartbeats longer than any of the other men.

Not wanting to call Dixon out or embarrass him in front of the other men, Megan said it went fine. "Arthur offered to go back on Tuesday and help install the temporary power line." She arched her brows, hoping Jerod would see the significance of this offer.

Jerod grinned and put a friendly hand on Arthur's shoulder. "Thanks, man. That's very nice of you. We can add that to your community service hours for this month."

Arthur waved a hand. "Think nothing of it. I can handle this sort of power line in my sleep. I also wanted to inspect all of the generators and make sure they have them all hooked up right so that next time they have an issue with power, the generators will kick in automatically." He scratched his chin. "I didn't like how long it took to get the power back on. There were quite a few people who had a tough time with the darkness."

"Thankfully, no one was injured." Megan had inquired with Sadie and Cody about that before she left, and both of them assured her there wasn't anything worse than a baby crying or someone dropping their food from the surprise.

She had looked for Daniel, but when she saw Cody she'd decided that it would be better to talk to him instead.

Not that she was avoiding the handsome cowboy.

Chapter 9

Today was the day that Megan would be back at the farm. Daniel wasn't sure if she would stay there the entire time or if she'd just drop Arthur off and leave. But he was prepared to take her out on a sleigh ride.

On Saturday, he'd seen her eye the sleigh a few times with a wistful sort of glance and he knew she wanted to go on that ride. And it was his job to show her a good time. Plus, it would be a great opportunity to show her he could have a serious discussion. And if God was on his side, he'd keep his foot out of his mouth.

Daniel had to grin at that thought.

It was rare he had such a difficult time talking to a woman, but Megan was not your average cowgirl. She was someone Daniel really wanted to get to know. Not that he had much time for a girlfriend. But he could make a little bit of time for a girl who was a friend—if she felt the same way.

And the only way to find out was to spend some time alone with her and keep his words proper. It wasn't that he was improper, it was that his mouth got away from him when he couldn't think straight.

When Megan did show up, Daniel was waiting near the front gate by the side of the house. He wanted to see if Megan would get out of the truck or if she'd leave without even getting out. If he could only speak with her for a moment or two and let her know what he had planned, maybe she'd be up for it. And maybe he'd stick his foot in his mouth—again.

It really was too bad there wasn't a pill for foot-in-mouth disease.

A feeling of excitement coursed through his veins, and he forced himself to slowly walk toward the gate to greet both Megan and Arthur. "Howdy. It's really great of you to come out and help."

"My pleasure." Arthur looked around and grinned when he spotted the utility truck on the other side of the barn. "I'll just be heading over there." He took off without a backward glance.

"Yeah, sure…" Megan shook her head and almost snorted. "I guess I know where his head is at right now."

"Well, it's good for men to find out what they like and then be able to do it." Daniel looked at Arthur and wondered why he was at Crooked Arrow. He didn't seem to have freaked out the other day when the power went out. And he also didn't use anything to help him walk. While it was too cold outside to see the man's hands or arms, he was pretty sure the guy didn't have any prosthetics.

"Okay, so I'll go find Sadie and see what she could use help with." Megan started to walk away.

Daniel shook his mind to get thoughts about Arthur out of his head. "Wait, I was thinking now would be the perfect time to show you the farm."

Thin lines appeared on Megan's brow and she stared at him. "What are you talking about? I've already seen the farm several times now."

Daniel held up a finger. "Ah, but you haven't seen the trees or taken advantage of the views afforded on a sleigh." He arched one brow as he waited for it to sink in.

She blinked.

"A sleigh ride. Do you remember when we spoke about it previously? You had said you wanted to see the farm from that angle." He was sure they'd spoken about it before, and she seemed excited to see it all while riding slowly through the trees on a horse-drawn sleigh.

"Oh, yes. I remember. But I've already been on one. Dana and I took a ride this weekend when Mike was leading the horse." Megan tilted her head and looked at Daniel as his face fell.

"Oh. Sorry. I thought we were going to do it." Daniel pursed his lips and kicked at a small snowball that had frozen over and was sitting at his feet. "Together."

"Well"—she drew out the word as she looked toward the fields and fields of trees—"I guess I haven't seen the trees during the day. We saw it just as the sun was setting and everything was fairly dark." Megan moistened her lips and considered for a moment longer. "If you wanted to show me the trees that aren't a regular part of the sleigh ride, that might be interesting."

Daniel stood tall and grinned. "My lady." He bent at the waist and motioned for her to walk before him toward the barn that held the draft horses who pulled the sleigh.

"Thank you." Megan's eyes narrowed, but she slowed her pace until Daniel was walking beside her.

On the other side of the barn sat a red sleigh with gold-and-black trim. On its side was the tree farm's logo in red and green on a white square backdrop. It was simple, but it worked well with the various items they sold at the gift shop, especially the canvas tote bags.

This sleigh wasn't the one the customers rode in, as it was designed for two people to ride. One of the riders would direct the horse while the other sat there looking at the winter wonderland as they passed by the snow-covered trees.

Daniel went inside the barn and brought out one brown horse with tan spots so dark they almost blended in with the brown. The horse was swooshing its tail back and forth and snorted a couple of times before he had the beast harnessed into the sleigh.

"My lady." Daniel held a hand out to help Megan get into the sleigh.

She grinned and put her hand in his as she stepped up. Before Megan sat down, she noticed a red-and-white checked blanket and unfolded it. The snow had stopped coming down earlier in the morning, but there was a little bit of wetness still on the seat. The blanked was laid down for them both to sit on.

"Oh, I almost forgot." He ran back to the barn and returned with a snowy white fur lap blanket. When Daniel got in and put the blanket on Megan's lap, she looked up to him with a real smile that touched him all the way to his toes.

"Thank you. This is perfect." Megan wrapped her gloved hands in the blanket and looked out to the snow-covered ground in front of them. Not realizing what she was doing, Megan scooched closer to Daniel.

Feeling the warmth of Megan next to him, Daniel smiled to himself. He took the reins and signaled for the horse to move forward. At first they rode in companionable silence while Megan looked out at the trees and the snowy wonderland. Overnight they'd received almost a foot of new snow, and the Christmas trees were covered with the glistening evidence of the storm.

He took a path that wasn't included in the normal tour loop. Instead, he guided the horse to the far back of the property, where they had a few giant trees they were holding on to for the future needs of their town. Cody supplied several towns with their annual Christmas trees, and they always wanted the largest trees on the farm. Close to twenty years earlier, Cody's father had set aside this section to grow the giant trees for the various cities. Even some of the larger ranch and farmhouses sported their giant trees.

"What kind of trees are those?" Megan pointed to a twenty-five-foot-tall Christmas tree with a bluish tint.

"That's a blue spruce. They're pretty popular trees. They keep their needles quite well, which makes for a good public tree. And they also have a natural conical shape, so trimming them is very easy." Daniel didn't want to mention that if you crushed up enough of the needles it started to stink, but that wasn't really a necessary point anyway.

"We have about an acre of these trees set aside to keep growing. We'll take out a few each year to sell, but then we always plant at least one more tree, sometimes two. Next spring we'll end up planting about one and a half trees for every tree we sold this year." They had to keep a good ratio of new trees to sold trees. Not all trees planted survived, but they also needed to build up inventory. If this year's pre-sales were anything to go by, they'd be selling more live trees in the years to come than they had in a decade.

They drove to the next stand of trees and Megan asked again. "Sorry, I love live trees, but I've never really thought about what type they were. I just picked out what I liked from a lot of pre-cut trees. I've never even chopped a tree down before."

"Really? Then you have to come back when the ranch is ready for a tree. I'll help you pick one out and you can chop it down yourself."

Megan flexed her muscles, but with a big bulky coat on it looked more like she was pointing in an odd way. "Sorry, that didn't work as well as I had thought it might."

Daniel chuckled, then held up one arm while the other held the horse's reins. When he flexed, his Carhartt jacket tightened around his biceps and he grinned. "I eat plenty of spinach, toot toot."

Megan furrowed her brow and scrunched her nose. "What does spinach have to do with biceps?"

"You know, Popeye?" He nodded, expecting her to get the cultural reference. Sure, it wasn't something his generation watched, but his Uncle Steve used to make the jokes all the time when Daniel was growing up.

"Um, who's Popeye?"

Daniel slapped his hand to his face. "You're kidding, right?"

She shook her head.

"How old are you? Fifteen?" Daniel chuckled and then stopped when he felt Megan stiffen next to him. He'd done it again—said something stupid.

Megan crossed her arms over her chest. "You know, we should probably head back in now."

He sat back against the bench seat of the sleigh. "I'm sorry, Megan. That was a lame joke. Foot-in-mouth disease strikes again."

They sat there in an uncomfortable silence as Daniel brought the sleigh down to the edge of the stand of trees and began to turn the horse around.

"Who is this Popeye?"

"I guess it makes sense you wouldn't know who he is. Out here on the farms and ranches we don't get much TV. It's mostly whatever we can get over the antenna." Daniel knew kids who had giant satellite dishes in their backyards and got over two thousand channels while he was growing up, but they never did. They were lucky to get the Saturday afternoon cartoons from the local TV station in Missoula.

She scrunched her nose. "Really? You didn't have the Disney Channel or Cartoon Network as a kid?"

He shook his head. "Nope. So I grew up watching local cable access cartoons, most of which were just repeats of what our parents and grandparents watched as kids. I had *Sesame Street* as a little boy, but then I started watching *He-Man* and *Popeye* along with *Bugs Bunny*. Some of the cartoons I watched as a kid were hand-drawn, like *Popeye*. He was a sailor who ate cans and cans of spinach which gave him these massive biceps. He always beat up the biggest bully on the show. Sometimes his arms even looked like the hammer you use to ring the bell at that game they still have at the fair. You know, the one only strong men can win?"

Megan's giggle sounded like tinkling glass and warmed Daniel's soul. She unfolded her arms and turned toward him. "Really? Like a giant mallet?"

"Yup. There was always some sort of good message for kids, but also a lot of beating up on the bad guys. They always lost, even if they were three times the size of the good guy." Images of Popeye, a short sailor who always had a corn-cob pipe in his mouth, flashed through Daniel's memory and he thought back to easier days. Days when he didn't care if a girl would even talk to him, let alone like him.

"And to think I grew up watching cartoons like *The Simpsons* and *Phineas and Ferb*." Megan giggled into her hand. "Just between us, I still watch *Phineas and Ferb* sometimes."

"It's alright. One year for Christmas my uncle bought me a DVD full of the old *Popeye* cartoons. And another year, he bought me a ten-disc set of old *Looney Tunes*. I think my favorite are still the ones with the Road Runner. He always gave it to Wile E. Coyote." Daniel chuckled. "Those were the days."

"Did you ever watch the Christmas cartoons?" Megan turned back to looking out and enjoying the different trees they drove past.

"What do you mean 'did?' I still do." Daniel turned his million-watt smile on Megan and winked.

"Ugh, why do you do that?" She threw her hands in the air and looked away from him.

"Do what?"

"Wink at me like you're God's gift or something?" The cold wall that had been coming down was now back up, and even higher and thicker than before.

Daniel sighed. When would he ever learn?

Chapter 10

S he should have known. Every time she started to warm up toward Daniel he went and said or did something totally idiotic. Why in the world would any man in this day and age think a woman would like him to wink at her? It would be one thing if he was a boyfriend or even a guy friend, but someone she barely even knew? That was uncalled for. It was downright degrading.

But there was something about Daniel that made Megan think he wasn't trying to be rude. He had said something about foot-in-mouth disease. Was it really that innocent? Could he just be inexperienced with talking to women?

When the sleigh ride first began and Daniel was telling her all about the different tree types that they grew and the interesting facts about needle retention, she thought he was quite charming. Then he said a few things that turned her off. Thinking back now, what he'd said wasn't too bad. Now that she was thinking about it, he did give off an awkward vibe, like he was really trying too hard to impress her. Well, except for when he talked about the trees. Then he was all ease and confidence.

Those moments were precious. His eyes glowed with excitement and he smiled from ear to ear. It wasn't a lecherous smile, either. It was a warm smile that reminded Megan of a sunny day on the beach. It filled her entire being with sunshine and sandy snowmen all at once.

Growing up on the California coast, Megan had more sand angels and sandmen than she did snow angels or snowmen. Most of her Christmases were spent in shorts and tank tops instead of parkas and snow boots. She had even heard some women talk about taking out their jeans lined with flannel this week. Who had ever heard of such a thing?

Then, when she saw a pair in the general store and she ran her hands along the inside, she'd bought them for herself. Thanks to those women she'd overheard, she was wearing comfortable and warm jeans at that very moment. Who knew flannel jeans would be so soft and comfortable? While she hadn't done it yet, she was tempted to buy a flannel shirt to wear around the ranch.

They had stayed silent for the rest of the ride back to the barn. When Daniel jumped down from the sleigh, he held out his hand to help Megan. "I'm sorry for saying stupid things."

Megan wasn't sure what to think of this cowboy, but her lips turned up slightly. "Thank you for showing me the trees. They really are beautiful."

"I'm glad you liked them. My offer still stands."

Her eyes narrowed. "What offer?"

"To help you pick out a tree when you're ready." Not waiting for a reply, Daniel walked on with the horse and sleigh so he could unhitch the horse and put her away for a rest, and some extra oats for a job well done.

Megan walked away, confused by the cowboy. One moment he was saying and doing stupid things, then the next he was being sweet and helpful. Would she ever understand men? Probably not.

Her mind was all discombobulated for the rest of the day. She was grateful she didn't have any one-on-ones with the guests that day. Although, she did have a group meeting that evening after dinner. Because her mind had been so all over the place since she'd left Daniel and the Big Sky Christmas Tree Farm, she decided she needed a few minutes with God before the meeting.

She sat alone in her room in the staff wing of the ranch house. It had been built back when ranchers had a lot of children as well as live-in help. Their ranch house boasted a total of ten bedrooms in the house along with two large outbuildings. One was where she held the group meetings, and the other was a sort of bunkhouse that could hold a dozen cowboys. The old ranchers would hire some year-round employees, but they'd also bring in seasonal help—cowboys who traveled around and helped ranchers bring in the herds for market, or harvest crops.

The previous ranch, when it was first built, must have had upwards of several thousand acres to be so large and have the ability to hire so many staff. It even came with two large barns. Currently they used one barn for storage and the other housed the few animals Jerod had. There were plans for expansion if funding came through. Funding was always an issue for non-profits like this one. If only they could find a large corporation or billionaire who would become their benefactor. But sadly, people didn't donate like they used to.

And lately, returning warriors and veterans weren't treated with the respect they deserved. Somehow society was turning on the military, like they did back in the seventies at the end of the Vietnam War. Not that Megan had experienced that scene. You know, since she hadn't been born yet.

Before her thoughts could become even more maudlin, she sat down with her Bible to pray. Sometimes, after a heartfelt prayer, God would instill a verse in her heart. She wanted to be able to look it up if He directed her to one. She needed His comfort and direction. Some of her guys were getting better with the treatment they offered at the ranch, and others like Sam weren't.

To be fair, Sam was a tad bit better than when she arrived. But of all the patients she'd ever worked with, he was making the least progress. That combined with her confusing time with Daniel had her mind going all over the place. And of course the events happening lately with the military didn't help her mind to focus, either.

God, I love you and I know you love me. Thank you for saving me and for helping me to find my calling and ministry. But Lord, I don't understand so many things right now. I need your guidance and help, as well as some peace. My soul is crying out for the innocent people destroyed by wars and governments taking advantage of their people. But I'm also so worried for my little tiny corner of the world right here. Does that make me a bad person? Should I worry more for the world at large? Should I worry at all?

A feeling of peace began to flow over Megan as she sat there, silently waiting for God's reply to her call for help. She itched to say more to God, to ask for exactly what she wanted. However, after being a Christian for so long she'd learned to wait and listen for God's word. And to want to bring her desires into God's will.

"Sometimes God gives us exactly what we want, but sometimes what we want isn't what's best for us." Megan's grandmother used to say that to her all the time. For the longest time she didn't understand what it meant. She was only a child when her grandmother passed, so it was only natural that she didn't learn what it truly meant until later on.

Megan's mother had learned that the hard way, and was still trying to learn the lesson. Although, Megan doubted she'd tried too much to learn it.

Not wanting to dwell on her mother, she turned her thoughts back to God and waited on His word. A passage began to take root in her mind and heart. That's when she knew it was from

God. When both her heart and her mind were in sync, it almost always meant that the Holy Spirit was directing a message at her. When she was younger, she tried to use that way of thinking when she wanted to do something she shouldn't, like sneak out of the house in the middle of night to meet up with friends.

Her heart and mind were in sync, but Megan also knew that it went against the rules her mother had set for her. The Bible was clear about obeying one's parents. It didn't matter what her mother was up to, she was supposed to follow the rules: go to bed at a certain time and stay in bed—alone, all night long. As well as a handful of others. Sadly, Megan didn't always do as her mother said. Most of the time she ignored her mom's rules and did whatever she wanted. Her mom was rarely around while Megan was in high school, so it wasn't like she'd know.

But later, Megan learned that if her heart and mind were in sync and the idea followed the Bible, then it was most likely from God.

She pulled the Bible from the table next to her bed where she'd laid it down before she began to pray and opened it up to Philippians chapter four. While she wasn't certain which verse she was supposed to pay attention to, she knew it was a short chapter, so she started on verse one and read until something stabbed at her heart.

Be careful for nothing: but in every thing by prayer and supplication with thanksgiving let your requests be made known unto God. And the peace of God, which passeth all understanding, shall keep your hearts and minds through Christ Jesus. – Phil 4:6-7.

Megan read the passage two more times and then thought about it. Megan had been worried about a lot of different things lately, and not just the guys at the ranch. Her mom was going through a rough patch and the world at large was going crazy.

Politics had divided the world. If you belonged to one side, the other hated you.

From what Megan had seen lately, mankind was heading down a path of death and destruction that wasn't too different from when the world went to war both times in the last century. Freedom to believe differently from those in power meant social ostracism at the very least, thanks to cancel culture. And in some cases it meant beatings or death.

But what could Megan do to change the world? Could one person make a difference?

YES, a voice boomed within her, and she jolted upright.

That was going to take some unpacking. And she didn't have time to get into what the Lord might want her to know. She had to get to her group meeting in the barn. Instead of feeling down and overwhelmed, Megan knew she had a purpose and God was going to use her to help heal those around her.

Maybe one of the wounded vets she healed would go on to become the next president, or start a company that would change the world. Was that what God was trying to tell her? Keep going, help those He put in her path, and the world just might begin to change—for the better.

With a renewed sense of duty and a heart full of peace and love, she made her way to the group session.

Chapter 11

"Are you sure we should do this?" Grandpops asked while chewing on his bare gums.

"Yes, he needs his sleep. And you know Cody, he'll be up with his alarm and working, no matter what the doctor said." Daniel had heard all about what happened the night before and he'd come over extra early that day.

It was the day after the sleigh ride with Megan, and Daniel was already working the farm well before the sun had even thought about casting a warm glow on their part of the Earth.

The night before, Cody'd been in an *almost* car accident. Someone had slid on ice and hit his truck while he and Sadie stood off to the side. Cody fell down on top of her when his truck hit him from the backside. They both got out of the way of the truck, but the fall to ground did damage to them both.

Grandpops had decided to let Cody sleep. But it was Daniel who suggested something he knew would come back to bite him in the saddle.

"I'll sneak in there if you want and turn off his alarm. He can get mad at me instead of you." There was no need for Joseph Makinaw to feel the brunt of Cody's ire; Daniel could take it very easily.

Somehow, Jerod heard all about the accident as well. In a small town like this, the rumor mill was more active than Santa's naughty-or-nice list. Megan had brought a few of the guys to the farm before it opened and all were helping out. Sam had been assigned the job of clearing the snow from the pathways inside the tree farm. While it did snow overnight, it wasn't too bad for parking trucks or cars that would have either four-wheel drive, snow tires, or chains.

Cody and Megan had worked out some sort of payment for the guys who helped out recently, but they wouldn't get an actual check until the money started coming in, which Daniel thought was ingenious. Thanks to everyone's help, and God's great blessings, word was out about the tree farm and people were coming from far and wide to see it. The cash was flowing.

If this kept up, Daniel knew the tree farm would be saved, along with his job, and the men from the Crooked Arrow would get a nice paycheck. It had to make them feel good to be able to earn an income, especially since so many of them had physical disabilities in addition to their mental ones. PTSD was real, and it could paralyze a warrior with fear. But putting in a hard day's work seemed to ease the mental pain just a bit. It also gave good men a sense of being needed.

There was something about being home and the horrors of war still halfway across the planet that caused men and women who didn't bat an eye while in the thick of it to drop and curl up into a ball when explosions sounded at home—like fireworks or a breaker being blown. Daniel had seen how a couple of ranchers who lived in the area reacted to a Fourth of July fireworks display in Bozeman a couple of years ago. He knew those men fought with valor and honor when they were in-country, but they had a tough time coming home.

Daniel had heard an explanation that made sense. When a warrior was in the thick of it, their bodies worked on instinct and their will to survive kept them moving. But once they were home, something in them told them they were safe and their minds needed time to acclimate and deal with what they had seen and done. This took a lot of time and patience.

So when a trigger event happened, they didn't act like the heroes they were. They became scared little boys and girls. Not because they weren't brave, but because their minds were still trying to process the horrors they went through. With some help and understanding, they could process it all in time. But sadly, too many didn't understand this and taunted someone who suffered from PTSD. On social media, he'd even seen civilians who had never served scoffing at the idea of PTSD being real.

Once, while at a rodeo in Las Vegas, Daniel had come across a group of young men jeering and throwing stuff at a soldier crouching behind a trash can after an old beater of a car passing him on the street had backfired. It was all Daniel could do to keep himself from teaching those boys a thing or two.

Then there were the returning heroes who couldn't stop drinking or doing drugs. They eventually let their anger get the best of them and hurt other people, or themselves. If only society, and politicians, took PTSD more seriously. But he guessed that was why places like Crooked Arrow Ranch were popping up left and right across the country. Non-profit groups were finding funding to help as many returning heroes as they could. Even the VA was starting to help more.

When Megan walked up to Daniel, he remembered what he had read in the paper that morning. "Megan, did you hear about the VA starting up a new grant fund for organizations dedicated to helping injured veterans heal and make the transition back to a civilian life?"

"Yes, I read that same article this morning. I went online and bookmarked the page that had the information. Tonight after dinner, I'm going to fill out the forms and see if we can get some more funding for the other projects we have planned." Megan smiled warmly at Daniel.

He wondered if she had forgiven him for the stupid comment he'd made the day before. Instead of asking, he decided to let it go and move forward.

"That's great." He nodded in approval. "If you need any help, please don't be afraid to ask. I may not have your experience or training, or but I do know a thing or two about working on a farm and a ranch."

Megan put a hand on his arm. "Thank you. I appreciate that." She pulled her hand back and clapped her gloved hands. "But for now, feel free to put me to work wherever you need help. And these guys"—she pointed to the other men she had brought with her—"are going to head out and see about crowd control for when you open the doors today."

"Perfect." Daniel nodded to the men, who grunted in response.

Only Skeeter, being the sociable guy he was, waved. "Hey, Daniel. Good morning."

"Good morning, Skeeter. Are you ready to greet everyone today?" Daniel and Megan had discussed what might be the best place for Skeeter. With his bubbly personality, they thought he'd make for a good greeter, information guy. They had a vest all ready for him, too. It wasn't anything fancy; just had that funny information logo on the back with a Big Sky Christmas logo on the front chest. Just to make sure everyone knew he worked for the tree farm, even though he was going to be sitting on a stool or hobbling around a bit on his crutches.

"You betcha. I can't wait to greet all the pretty cowgirls." Skeeter grinned and looked at Sam. "See, if you were a bit nicer you could flirt with all the pretty girls, too."

Sam growled. "I don't wanna flirt with anyone." He turned around and went back to blowing the snow along the pathway they were on.

Daniel wished there was a way to break down those walls that Sam had built up around him. They were so tall and thick that not even a thief could scale them. He doubted a cannonball could even dent them. Maybe a trebuchet with a flaming ball could do it? He'd have to find something to help Megan with this guy.

Megan rolled her eyes at Skeeter. "Dude, just be cool. Don't go all girl-crazy on us."

Skeeter held up one hand while he leaned on his crutches. "Hey, I can't help it if all the pretty girls like to chat me up." He winked at Megan.

Daniel watched her reaction to Skeeter's wink. It was nothing like how she reacted to his. She shook her head and lightly slapped the back of his head but said nothing. Why was it that when Skeeter winked at her it was all one big joke, but when he did it she looked as though she wanted to sock him one? Women, pft. He'd never understand them.

Maybe Sam had the right of it.

Before Daniel had a chance to ask her about it, Javier, one of their regular workers, walked up to Daniel. Javier tipped his hat toward Megan. "Ma'am." Then he looked at Daniel. "Boss, we've got a problem in the back lot, near the Frasier firs."

"What sort of problem?" All thoughts of Megan and flirting flew out the window. Daniel was now focused on the farm. Cody was still in bed sleeping where he ought to be, so that left Daniel in charge.

"I was out with the tractor cutting a few more trees and I heard barking. Like a lot of barking." Javier's eyebrows rose and he quickly looked at Megan before turning his attention back to Daniel. "There's something out there."

Daniel sighed and ran a hand down his face. It wouldn't be the first time they'd had wild animals in the tree farm; their fencing wasn't exactly built to keep everything out. But it usually meant a lot of extra work for them. And with the crowds they'd been experiencing, now really wasn't the time to deal with this. "Alright, I'll head out on a four-wheeler."

"I'll lead the way. I still need to collect those trees, so I'll be on the tractor." Javier began to walk away.

"Wait. I want to help," Megan called out.

Daniel's stomach soured, and he winced. It wasn't that he didn't want her company, because he really did like having her around. It was more that he wasn't sure what they were going to find out there. "It might be something gruesome."

Megan chuckled. "What? Like a bear?"

Daniel shook his head. "No, the bears are hibernating right now." Over the years they'd seen their fair share of bears coming on the property, but it was usually during the drier years, when food was scarce. Or the huckleberry season seemed to sprout up right in their back fields. Three things he'd learned early on: carry a rifle, bear spray, and always have a guard when harvesting huckleberries. Those seemed to attract the bears like moths to a flame.

"Sooo…" Megan trailed off as she waited for his explanation.

"Boss, I didn't see anything large out there, just heard the dogs going crazy. As long as she stays close, it should be fine." Javier waved them on. He seemed anxious to get going.

They walked through the barn and into the tack room, where they had a locked office with a gun safe. Most of the farm's shotguns and rifles were inside the house, but they did keep a few locked up in the barn just in case.

Grandpops Makinaw came running into the barn wheezing. "I just got…a…call." He leaned over and put his hands on his knees.

"Joseph, what's wrong? Is Cody alright?" Daniel went to the man and helped him into a chair.

Mr. Makinaw waved Daniel away. "I'm fine. Just fine. So is Cody." He tried to smile, but the old man hadn't put his dentures in yet. Cody was forever going off on his grandpops to wear his teeth from the moment he got up until he got into bed. But the old man hated them and most of the time chose to ignore Cody's pleading.

"Then what's wrong?" Daniel knew something was up, but Joseph was taking forever to get the words out.

With a deep sigh, Joseph relayed the phone call from their neighbor. "There's a trail of animal parts out along the borders to our ranches and his dogs got loose."

"Ah, yes. We were just getting ready to check out the commotion that Javier heard not too long ago." Daniel felt easier and went to open the safe containing the rifles. He also pulled down a bag that held bear spray, just in case. It worked on more than just bears.

"I'm coming with you." Joseph stood up and swayed.

Megan jumped to his rescue and looked at Daniel with pleading eyes.

"No, you need to stay here." Daniel wasn't about to let this old man go with them only to have him drop from a heart attack. Cody would kill him.

"Young man, this is my property and you work for me. Not the other way around." From a sitting position, Joseph arched a brow and glared.

Daniel stopped himself from giving him a retort about old people. Then knew exactly what to say. "Who'd keep an eye on the tree farm if we were gone for hours? Someone has to manage the place—it's going to open in about fifteen minutes."

Joseph gnawed on his naked gums. "You have a point." He waved a dismissive hand. "Alright, you win this round." This time when Joseph stood, he didn't wobble.

"Oh, and Grandpops, please put your teeth in. You know how it freaks out the customers, especially the kids, when you don't have them in." Daniel tried to hide his grin, but it came out with his chuckle.

Grumbling something about ungrateful whippersnappers, Joseph left the others in the barn and made his way back out toward the front of the tree farm.

Megan watched the old man leave. "Does he do that often?"

"What, grumble? Don't all old men?" Daniel checked the barrels of the rifles and took a leather satchel down from the pegs on the wall.

She shook her head. "No, forget to put his dentures in when he leaves the house."

Javier let out a full-bellied laugh. Almost like a Santa bellow, but since Javier was skinny it came out as more of a shrill sound. "He always, and I mean *always*, does that."

Daniel chuckled and grabbed the rest of their gear.

Chapter 12

When Daniel first suggested they take the sleigh instead of his plan to ride out on the four-wheeler, Megan about scoffed at the idea that Daniel didn't think she could ride a four-wheeler. But when he explained that it helped save gas to take the sleigh, and would be much more comfortable for them both since they only had the one four-wheeler, Megan felt like an idiot.

Daniel had never made her feel like an incompetent woman before; she wasn't sure where this feeling was coming from now. So many men had just assumed she didn't know how to do one thing or another because she was a woman, but her time in the Army had taught her how to drive many different vehicles. And besides, when she was in high school she hung out with a crowd of boys and girls who all had ATVs. She even knew how to ride a motorcycle.

Wouldn't that cause a few eyes to shoot up if she rode a Harley down the road? Not that driving a motorcycle ever really interested her, but it would be fun to rent one and drive around sometime, just to show that she could do something different.

Megan hated it when anyone, including women, assumed that all women couldn't do anything a man could do. Well, alright, making yellow snow might not be as easy or comfortable for a woman, but really, what woman *wanted* to do it? There were some differences between the sexes that Megan was grateful for. She'd never been interested in peeing contests. Just the idea of them grossed her out. But boys will be boys.

She only hoped she wasn't within earshot the next time anyone wanted to see how far they could make the snow yellow. Waves of disgust rolled up and down her back, and she shivered.

"Hey, you gonna get on or what?" Daniel said as he waited next to the sleigh.

Megan licked her lips. "Of course." She had enjoyed the last sleigh ride they'd taken, until he made a wrong comment. Would today be the same, or would Daniel be able to keep from sticking his foot in his mouth?

When she sat next to him on the small front bench, she had to sit right up against him. Daniel had put the supplies on his other side and he sat mostly in the middle of the bench. Which didn't leave her much room.

"Here." Daniel draped a warm, thick blanket over her legs. "This should help keep you warm on the ride."

A feeling of warmth spread through her and she realized that she did enjoy sleigh rides with this cowboy. There were times he was such a gentleman and everything seemed so easy between them, like now.

They all slowly departed the tree farm area. The lot had just opened up and hordes of people were already spilling in from all over. They had to move slowly so as not to hit anyone.

However, they were able to pick up some speed once they cleared the general area. They still had to be careful as it was a pick-your-own-tree sort of farm, and who knew how far anyone would go into the rows and rows of Christmas trees to find the perfect one?

Megan noted that the ground nearest the gift shop area, where the trees were paid for, had an assortment of various trees growing in all different sizes. There were Douglas fir trees, noble firs, blue spruces, and a few she wasn't quite sure about the names of. All of them had saplings, three-footers, and anything else up to eight feet. But she didn't see any of the tags that denoted a tree above eight feet tall.

Cody and his family must have decided that this would be the best place to grow the majority of the pick-your-own-and-cut-it-down trees. It was a large plot of land, but it was also the closest area to the heart of the farm's activities.

Once they cleared that lot, a sign denoted that they were entering the forest of Leyland cypress trees. Megan liked these trees. They weren't the typical Christmas tree; they looked more like what you'd find growing on a fine estate. But if her memory served, they didn't have a scent to them. While she wasn't allergic to any trees, she had known some people who were. This was the perfect tree for those with allergies. The snow didn't seem to stick as well to these branches since they stood up practically straight, and they had a feathery leaf instead of needles on a branch. Daniel had explained that these trees were preferred by those who hated having to clean up needles from around their trees all season long.

Behind that lot was a section for the blue spruce. She and Daniel had been in this section during their sleigh ride the other day. The memory warmed her, until she remembered his stupid comments. But he did seem more like he was inexperienced at talking to women than a typical jerk. Her hands tightened in her lap when she noticed the blood trails in the snow.

All thoughts of romance, ambiance, or foot-in-mouth disease flew from her mind. This was real. This was scary. Not as scary as her time in Afghanistan, but just as real. She hoped and prayed it was only animal blood and not human. Megan wasn't sure what she'd do if they found a mutilated human corpse out there. She knew that this far out, their cell phones didn't have coverage. Thankfully, she noticed that Daniel had a radio in his pack. They could call back to the house if there was any real danger.

Daniel stopped the horse and sleigh. "Aright, I think you should stay here with the sleigh. I'll go with Javier and check this out."

Her hackles were up, and she was about to lay into him for sidelining her just for being a woman when he held up his hands.

"I can see the anger in your eyes. This isn't because you're a woman, it's because you're green."

Her shoulders that had been pulled back slunk forward, and her retort died on her tongue. "Green?" She didn't think she looked as though she was about to puke, did she?

"This is your first time having to deal with animal mutilations, right?" Daniel's voice was soft and he put a hand on her arm.

When he was sweet and caring like this, she forgot all about foot-in-mouth disease and leaned into his warmth. "I've seen worse than a bloody animal corpse."

His lips pursed and he drew in a breath. "I don't doubt it. But I want to make sure I know what we're dealing with first. The dogs are still barking, so the animal—or animals—might still be nearby. If they are, I'm gonna have to shoot to kill." He squeezed her arm. "Will you be alright with that?"

Her eyelids fluttered and she sucked in a quick breath. Since leaving the Army she hadn't been near any sort of gunshots. And she knew from her own experience that the report from a rifle in close proximity would be loud and jarring. "If a carnivore is out here on your lands killing other animals, then you do what you need to."

"Alright, does that mean you want to stay back?" Daniel lowered his head and looked directly in her eyes.

The action was intimate, like a lover checking on his sweetheart. For some reason it gave her strength she didn't think she had. When she'd signed on to the Crooked Arrow Ranch to be their counselor, she'd specifically asked about guns. Jerod had told her they did have to carry rifles when out on the land, but so far he hadn't needed to fire one at all. They did have a firing range, but it was in the very back of the land, specifically designed so the sounds wouldn't set off any of the guests who might not like to hear gunshots.

The one thing that was consistent in her nightmares, besides the sounds of dying friends, was gunshots. Sometimes they were so loud and vivid in her dreams, she'd wake in a cold sweat with a sore throat.

She also knew from her training that she would eventually have to confront her last fear. Now was as good a time as any. She couldn't afford to break down in front of any of her patients. But doing it front of Daniel, while extremely embarrassing, would be better in the long run.

Megan stood taller and backed up so he wasn't touching her anymore. "Yes, I can do this." She wasn't about to ask for a gun, not yet. But she would go with Daniel and deal with anything that came their way.

She was stronger than she knew.

But when they followed the trail, she wished she hadn't gone with them.

Red, green, and white were Christmas colors, but she knew that no one ever thought of arranging anything like this for Christmas. Megan hated even associating this shade of color with one of her favorite holidays.

The saplings would have to be destroyed; she knew enough about scents and wild animals to understand that you couldn't completely remove the scent of blood from a tree.

But thankfully, no warning bells went off in her head. She wasn't about to puke or do anything truly embarrassing like faint. However, she was saddened by what appeared to have been a coyote dinner party on a small pack of wild animals. The remains of rabbits and a deer were left behind.

"Poor Bambi." Daniel shook his head.

"What?" Megan slapped his arm. What was with him and inappropriate comments?

"Hey, what's wrong? It was a fawn." With furrowed brows, he glared at her.

"Really, you don't see how wrong that comment was?" Megan rolled her eyes and shook her head. "Men."

"Sorry." Daniel's shoulders hunched and he put his gloved hands into the pockets of his jacket.

In this distance, she could hear the dogs barking. It was a different sound from coyotes. She would never forget the first night she heard a pack of coyotes at the Crooked Arrow Ranch. It woke her up in the middle of the night and she could have sworn it was a pack of hyenas yipping and howling instead of coyotes. She had always thought they either sounded like dogs or wolves. She would have preferred to keep thinking that.

Reality sometimes wasn't a friend.

A chill ran down her spine as she remembered the haunting melody of that first pack. Later, when she heard the sound again, she remembered being frustrated by being woken up at three in the morning. Now she usually slept through their yipping and howling.

But out here, no one would have heard the sounds of the coyotes all excited and worked up over a meal such as this. While it was disgusting, it was also a part of nature. Mankind would never be able to stop animals from acting the way they were created to act.

"So, what do we do now?" Megan looked around at the mess and hoped none of the guests would make their way out here. "Families don't come out this far, do they?"

Daniel looked up and eyed the surrounding trees. "Actually, they do. But if we hurry we can cordon off this section and then clean it up." He directed Javier to get the closed tape out and set a perimeter wide enough that no one would be able to see anything.

"I'll go and cover over the red snow," Megan offered.

"Actually, we'll need to shovel it up and burn it after we burn the carcasses. It's best to make sure it doesn't show up should the temperature turn and the snow melt." Daniel ran a hand down his face and sighed. "And besides, when boots start to walk all over this place the snow will be churned and it could easily be brought up to the top before the red has a chance to dissipate into the ground."

Megan felt her nose scrunch and a gurgling sounded in her stomach. Not the kind that meant she was hungry, just the opposite. Some winter wonderland this was turning out to be.

Thoughts of hiding this sight from children spurred her on. She went looking for kindling while Daniel gathered up the bits that needed to be burned.

"Someone is going to have to stay out here and keep an eye on the fire the entire time. We can't take a chance that any embers could spark a fire. While it's highly unlikely with all the snow, it is still a danger." Daniel looked at Javier.

"I'll stay out here and finish it up, boss. Why don't you and Megan head back and clean up?" Javier said.

"Thanks, I appreciate it." Daniel slapped his worker and friend on the shoulder and took Megan back.

It was a silent ride back to the hustle and bustle of the farm. Megan wasn't sure what to say, so she stayed quiet the whole ride. On the way out there she was mesmerized by the trees; now, she didn't even see them.

When they got off the sleigh, Daniel offered Megan the use of the house to clean up.

"Thanks, I think I'd like that. I feel like I need a long, hot shower." She shivered when she thought of what they had just done. But at the same time, she also felt as though she had done something really important. If anyone, especially kids, had found their way out there, it could have been a scary sight for them. And might have even turned into a social media nightmare for the tree farm.

After everything they had done—the guys posing for the calendar, opening up a craft fair, bringing in the carnival, and all the other little things—the farm could end up in a lot of trouble if a kid saw this and posted about it on social media. That was one of the worst parts about technology these days: anything and everything could hurt a business, or a person's reputation. Even something as natural as what had just happened could hurt Cody's farm if the wrong people saw it, or if it was shown in the wrong light.

Instead of taking a shower, Megan washed her face and her hands. Then she checked herself to make sure nothing was on her clothes. They were clean. Well as clean as they could be while out riding on a sleigh through the snow. She needed to get back outside and make sure her guys were all doing alright.

She'd ignore Daniel for now, although on closer inspection she realized he was only trying to lighten the mood with his Bambi comment. It just brought back a childhood memory she would rather not have had at that moment. Her only dog while she was growing up was named Bambi because she had the same coloring as the Disney character and was just as sweet. Her poor baby was run over by a car out front of their apartment complex, and she saw it all. But it wasn't just any random car, it was her mother's latest boyfriend. One she already hated.

No use in thinking about those bad days; she had some really good days ahead of her. This year, Christmas was going to be special for a change, as was Thanksgiving. She couldn't remember the last time she'd had a nice, homecooked turkey dinner with all the trimmings.

The Army turkey dinners weren't anything to write home about. Some days she actually preferred the MREs to the chow hall. The meals ready to eat (MRE) could be somewhat good. Some of the packs even had M&M's or Skittles. Those were the good ones.

This year, she wasn't just going to have a big dinner on Thanksgiving Day with everyone out at the ranch—on the Saturday after she would be attending the town's yearly Thanksgiving dinner. She'd never heard of an entire town getting together to celebrate a dinner like that.

The other day, when she and Daniel were discussing it, he had told her all about how everyone would bring a dish to share. "A few of the churches take turns making up the turkeys and ham. It's a tradition that goes all the way back to when our town was founded."

"Really? And it still goes on to this day?" Megan couldn't believe a small town did something like this all these years and no one seemed to tire of it.

He nodded. "Yup, there's always those out of town for the weekend, or some who get sick. But for the most part the entire town and the surrounding ranches and farms participate. We fill the community center to the brim. It's also the unofficial start to Christmas around here."

"How so?"

"Well, those who are in need can sign up for the giving tree. Parents who won't be able to afford gifts for their kids can fill out forms that end up as Christmas ornaments on the town's giving tree later in the week."

"I thought Lottie's decorations before Thanksgiving marked the unofficial start?" Megan chuckled.

"That's the Frenchtown Roasting Company's unofficial start. The town of Frenchtown begins their Christmas season right after Thanksgiving. That weekend the town's decorations go up, and by Monday the entire town is decorated to the hilt." Daniel grinned and rubbed his hands as he thought about all of the pumpkin spice lattes he'd be getting through the rest of the year.

Megan had thought she would attend the dinner with Daniel, but he hadn't asked her. They continued to bicker over one thing or another, usually because of sticking his foot in his mouth. So maybe that was why he hadn't asked her yet? Maybe she should stop taking offense at some of his more innocuous comments. None were truly meanspirited or said in a way that made her think he was *trying* to offend. It was just that they rubbed her wrong at times.

She doubted anyone else would have taken such offense at the Bambi joke. Most people would have laughed along with him. That really was her own personal issues coming up.

When her phone buzzed, she pulled it out of her coat pocket, frowned, and stuffed it back in. That was a call for another day.

"Sam, how goes it?" Megan walked around the grounds and noticed Sam and Mike were sitting at a picnic table having a hot cup of coffee.

A couple of women her age were sitting at a table looking at something and giggling as she approached. Their laughter caught her eye and she looked down. To her amusement, it was the Big Sky Christmas calendar. They had it open to the page with Javier posing. Of course he was fully clothed, but she hadn't realized that he could rope calves. Although, she hadn't really looked at it yet. She had planned to buy one the other day but didn't get around to it.

Since Jerod had posed for the calendar, she'd wanted to make sure they had at least a dozen all over the ranch. But she had heard some of the guys joking around with her boss and they'd mentioned the calendar. The guys had all bought several calendars the first day they were available.

Jerod was the May pin-up man. He was in a red truck with a field of sunflowers behind him. His denim shirt and black Stetson were the only clothing visible, but you could tell he was a cowboy. And a very handsome one at that, with a day's worth of scruff and a smile that pulled the viewer in. The photo of him looked as though he was used to being photographed. And it appeared he was very comfortable with his pose.

But in real life, any time one of those pictures showed up his face went beet red. Megan doubted he'd pose for the next calendar. Of course, he'd be married by the next one, so maybe that would disqualify him? Either way, she still needed to get her calendar to show her support for the farm. For no other reason, honestly.

Okay, maybe there was another reason to get the calendar. Sometimes, and only sometimes, Megan had a bit of a prankster in her.

Chapter 13

Daniel didn't know when he'd been so happy to see Cody. It wasn't often that Cody left him in charge during the Christmas season. While it wasn't technically the Christmas season until Friday, the craziness of the season had already started.

When he and Megan returned from taking care of the wild animal issue, there were a million things that needed taking care of. Megan had walked away saying she didn't want to be in his way, but she was never in his way. Something about her presence soothed him in a way no other had ever done. Daniel wanted her by his side.

Especially now.

Megan had a way about her that calmed the savage beast within men. Or at least, that's what it seemed like whenever he saw her interaction with the wilder men at the Crooked Arrow. Daniel could use that skill right about now.

A patron was complaining about not being allowed out in the back of the farm where she believed the best trees were kept for only the luckiest of customers. It just so happened it was the area Javier had to cordon off.

"Ma'am, I'm sorry you can't get back there right now. But I promise you, we aren't keeping you away on purpose. There was an incident with some wild animals and we have to clean it up. Once everything is back in order, the tape will come down and you can go back there." Daniel tried to give her a real smile, but he just couldn't. It wasn't even lunch yet and he was already exhausted.

"Mm-hm. I bet." The angry customer put her hands on her hips and leaned forward into Daniel's personal space. "You better not have allowed Hayley back there before I can go and get the best tree." She put a finger in his face. "You know she always tries to one-up me with her tree."

Daniel stepped back and put his hands in the air. "I can assure you, there are zero customers back there right now. No one pays to have a section cordoned off while they shop. We don't do that."

Snowballs, the audacity of these women and their need to one-up each other every year. Normally Cody dealt with these types of issues, and thanks to his grinch-like attitude the ladies cowered and moved off. Maybe he had the right of it.

The moment she walked away, another woman with murder in her eyes walked up. But so did Cody.

Daniel breathed a sigh of relief. "Hey, how ya feelin'?" Daniel grinned, but Cody glared.

"Excuse me, but I have a bone to pick. Who's in charge here?" A woman in her late fifties or early sixties put a fist in the air to punctuate her words.

Daniel pointed to Cody while Cody pointed to him.

"He owns the farm." Daniel grinned.

Cody smirked. "But he's the foreman."

It looked like Daniel's plan to let Cody sleep in was going to backfire on him. He could read the look in Cody's eyes, and that cowboy was out for blood. Too bad the grinch didn't turn his ire on the woman standing in front of them.

"Well, I don't care if one of you is Santa Claus himself. I'm angry."

"What's this? You don't care about being angry in front of Santa?" The town's resident Santa Claus walked up and put his hands on his belly and laughed. "Usually everyone wants to be on my nice list."

"Santa?" the woman spluttered. "But, but…ah…I mean… Judy, she started it all." The woman gulped and turned a confused look to Daniel. "Why did you rope off the best section for her?"

Daniel realized this must have been Hayley. He narrowed his eyes and glared at the woman. "Look, we don't play those games. There was a real issue back there today and it's not safe for anyone to walk around that area. Once it is, we'll open it back up and anyone can go in and pick out their tree."

Cody opened his mouth, but closed it when he saw his grandfather out of the corner of his eye. "You've got this." Not a question for Daniel, but more of an order. Then he headed toward the barn.

While Daniel was watching his friend hobble along, the woman was looking back and forth between him and Santa. He noticed the woman seemed confused, but still tried to get Daniel's attention. This time in a much more pleasant tone of voice.

He sighed and shook his head. "Mrs…?"

The woman gave him a shy smile and her eyes tilted to Santa, then back at him. "It's just Hayley. And how long do you think it will be before that section is open again?"

Daniel wanted to smirk, but instead he smiled and rubbed his chin. "I'd say after lunch sometime. It's going to take a while to clean up the area and make sure it's safe. Maybe two or three o'clock, I'd guess."

A steely glint of something, maybe anger, passed through the woman's eyes, but she took a moment to calm herself and then gave Daniel a terse nod. "I'll be here, waiting." Then she walked away after giving Santa a sweet smile.

"Ah, I'd say she was trying hard to be on her best behavior for you. She must have kids at home." Daniel rubbed the tight muscles in his neck. If things kept up like this, he'd be the one needing an Epsom salt bath that night and a long sleep.

"Ho, ho, ho. Even those without young children at home tend to be on their best behavior this time of year." Santa rubbed his belly. "Say, I hear you've got some of those famous scones Sadie makes. Would you mind pointing me in the right direction?"

He couldn't help it—Daniel's shoulders relaxed and he chuckled. No one could stay frustrated when Santa was around.

For the next hour Daniel kept looking for Megan everywhere he went, then he had to remind himself that she was busy with other things. Her job wasn't to spend her entire day on the farm. She had responsibilities back at her ranch. Even though he didn't see her leave, Daniel was sure she had left.

However, when lunchtime came around he decided he had to know for sure. Then he chided himself for wanting to spend all of his time with her. Not only did she have a job to do, which didn't include hanging around him all day long, he had work as well.

Cody had been ordered to the couch by his grandfather, and the two of them were responsible for making sure everything went smooth that day. So when he saw Skeeter across the paddock, his feet moved without any conscious direction from his brain. And when he was within talking distance of the man from the Crooked Arrow Ranch, who also happened to be the nicest guy he'd met so far, Daniel couldn't help what he did next.

"Hey, Skeeter. How goes it?" Daniel grinned at the smiling man dressed as a cowboy. Although to be fair, Skeeter had earned the right to be called a cowboy. He worked on a ranch, albeit not very strenuously, but he still helped with Jerod's small herd of cattle as well as various odds and ends at the ranch. And he also worked hard here on the farm, even with his crutches. The man didn't sit around bemoaning his injuries. Instead, he helped customers pick out trees, directed traffic, answered all sorts of questions, and didn't let one single customer get past him without smiling. Even the unhappy fathers and husbands who had been cajoled into spending too much of their hard-earned money on a tree that wouldn't last through New Year's Eve walked away from Skeeter with a smile.

"Right pleasant day today. Lots of nice people coming through with a smile and a handshake." Skeeter leaned against one crutch and put his hand out for Daniel to shake.

"I see you're in your regular good mood."

"Of course. With lovely ladies to flirt with everywhere I turn, what's not to smile about?" With his wicked grin, he turned to wink at a pretty young lady who smiled at Skeeter and completely ignored Daniel.

That was happening a lot lately. Used to be that Daniel was the one who had the women smiling at him and ignoring Cody. Had he turned into the grinch? No, that couldn't be it. "I see the ladies enjoy your attentions."

"It seems word got out about us cowboys from the Crooked Arrow. They know we're all veterans." Skeeter looked back and gave Daniel a devilish grin. "Women love a man in uniform."

"But you aren't in uniform." Daniel motioned up and down at what Skeeter was wearing and even noted his safety green vest.

Skeeter put up a finger. "Ah, but they can imagine me in my Class-A uniform, or even my BDUs." He waggled his brows.

Daniel furrowed his brows. "What's a BDU?"

"Battle Dress Uniform. Fancy name for camos."

"Ah, I see." And he did. One thing Daniel knew about women was they all loved a man in uniform. He saw it every Veteran's Day and even on the Fourth of July when residents donned their military uniforms for the parades. The women of Frenchtown always went wild for the servicemen. "But, are you also helping the men?" He arched a brow, expecting to hear some fluff.

"But of course. Most of the men are here with women, after all." Skeeter grinned.

Daniel should have known. Maybe he could get some pointers from one of the most popular men in town right now. But first, "Do you know where Megan is?"

A sly smiled crossed Skeeter's face. "Why? Do you have a question for our favorite counselor?"

"I was going to see if she wanted to join me for lunch." Daniel wasn't sure if he should trust Skeeter with that information, but the man was the only one who seemed to like Daniel.

Skeeter snorted. "She had to leave. I think she went into town to check on Sadie. You heard about the accident last night, right?"

Daniel nodded and sighed. He'd probably not see Megan until she came back to pick up the guys when the day was over. But it would be nice to hear how Sadie was doing.

"Will you ask her to come find me when she gets back?"

Before Skeeter could respond with any sort of joke, a couple of pretty cowgirls walked up with a question for Skeeter.

Daniel didn't know how a man on crutches could be so popular, but he was. Within just a few seconds the man was surrounded by beautiful women all wanting his attention. And Skeeter was soaking it up.

The only woman whose attention Daniel wanted wasn't anywhere near the tree farm at that moment.

Chapter 14

When the morning of Thanksgiving arrived, Megan was anything but thankful. She wished she was. Most people would be thrilled to be in her shoes. Here she was preparing a traditional Thanksgiving meal for all the men at the ranch. A couple had gone home to celebrate with their families, but the rest were there.

Even Dana Baker had come over to help. She and her family were joining the residents at the ranch that day. It wouldn't be long before Dana was the woman in charge. Once she married Jerod, she'd run the house and kitchen. But until then, Megan was the woman in charge.

They had a regular cook, but she was home with her family for the day. Megan wasn't sure what she'd been thinking when she told Mrs. Bertram she could take the entire day off. In fact, she even told the woman to leave early on Wednesday and not worry about preparing anything in advance for them, since she had her own family to care for. Not that any of them really needed her there to help; the woman's daughter-in-law would have it all under control. But Megan was feeling grateful yesterday, and blessed, so she let the cook leave early.

Now, she wasn't feeling grateful or blessed.

Dana was a big help, and the meal would be good, but she'd give anything to leave right then and there. Guilt was eating her up. She should have taken at least one of her mother's calls this past week, but she was so busy, and so happy. The thought of having to deal with her mother was just too much. Now, she was kicking herself.

"Megan?" Dana put a hand on her arm.

"Hm?" Megan frowned at the potatoes in front of her. None of them had been peeled yet, and it was getting a bit late for mashed potatoes if she wanted them peeled.

"What's wrong?" The barista put her bowl on the counter and stood facing Megan, waiting for a response.

"Nothing. Well, besides these mashed potatoes. I wish I would have gotten up earlier now." Megan sighed and picked up a potato. Turning it around, she glared at it.

"There's more going on than a desire to have mashed potatoes with their skins off. And in case you didn't know, keeping the skins on is healthier. The skin is where most of the nutrients are hiding." Dana took a couple of the potatoes that had already been washed and scrubbed. She began to cut them up in pieces and put them in the pot of water on the stove. "Here, help me chop them up. They'll heat faster and be easier to mash in smaller cubes."

"Right, sorry."

"Where are you, because you certainly aren't here on the Crooked Arrow Ranch." Dana stopped what she was doing and tilted her head as she watched Megan.

"Sorry, family problems. I'll get my head back into prep work." She gave her friend a quick smile and took a potato and began to cube it. Once she had a full cutting board, she moved the pieces to the pot.

Dana bit her lip. "Well, I'm here if you want to talk. I know you can't always talk about what's going on, but if this has nothing to do with your patients, then you really should open up to someone." She grinned. "A wise woman once told me that bottling up your issues isn't healthy."

A slow smile spread across Megan's face. "Gee, I wonder who that was?"

"Mrs. Claus," Dana deadpanned.

Both young women laughed.

Then Megan threw a small piece of potato at Dana.

"Hey, now. We have to clean the kitchen when we're done here, so don't go making a mess." Dana picked up the piece from the floor and dropped it in the trash can before washing her hands.

"Actually, the men will be doing the cleaning, since we're doing the cooking." Megan grinned and threw another piece at Dana.

The ensuing laughter and plunking of potatoes hitting the ground caused Jerod to come searching out the cause of the strange sounds in his kitchen.

"Hey, what's all this mess?" Jerod bellowed above the laughs and screeches.

Both women stopped in their tracks and tried to muffle their laughs. Megan snorted and Dana blanched.

Jerod looked around at the food on the ground and the mess the two women had made. "I hope you don't expect me or any of the other guys to clean this up." He put his hands on his hips and glared at the both of them as though they were little kids in trouble.

Dana crossed her arms over her chest and stuck her chin up in the air.

Megan laughed out loud. "Well, we are the ones doing all the work here. I'd say the men, and that includes you"—she pointed at Jerod— "can take turns cleaning up after us."

"For a change," Dana mumbled.

Jerod put his hands in the air in surrender. "Hey now, we don't mind cleaning up as long as we aren't cleaning up after your food fights."

"Food fight? Did someone say food fight?" Skeeter hobbled in on his crutches and grinned.

All three of them put their hands out. "No!"

Skeeter frowned and pulled back. "What? It looks like you already had a fun time without me."

"And they wasted about half a bag of potatoes in the process." Jerod glared at Megan.

"It wasn't all me, so I don't know why you're giving me the stink eye." Megan crossed her dirty arms over her chest, then felt a gooey mush seep through the arms of her shirt and uncrossed them. She looked down at her arms. "Gross."

Jerod pointed. "That's why. You look to be the culprit here, not my Dana." He walked over and put an arm around his fiancée. "Ugh. I take that back." He took two steps away. "What were you two thinking?"

The two women looked at each other sheepishly. "I guess we weren't?" Dana bent over to pick up a pile of potatoes at her feet.

"What made you two act like little kids?" Jerod asked.

Megan shrugged. "I don't know. Maybe it was just a way to blow off some steam?"

Jerod shook his head. "That's what horse riding, archery, mucking out stalls, and the plethora of other activities on a ranch are for." He looked between the two women. "Food isn't for wasting."

Megan felt guilty, again. She knew the ranch was operating on a shoestring budget and they didn't have the funds to waste food like this. She probably had wasted at least half a bag of potatoes. Luckily, it was one of their staples so they had a lot in the pantry. "I'll get more and clean them."

"I can help," Skeeter offered.

Megan smiled at the cowboy. He was always wanting to help. The man was one of the nicest guys she had ever met. Skeeter was going to make a fantastic husband to one lucky woman— once he was ready to settle down and stop flirting with anyone in a skirt and a pretty smile.

"I'll clean the floor of our mess if you want to clean the potatoes?" Dana asked.

"Sounds good to me." Skeeter grinned, ambled over to the sink, and waited for the pile of potatoes Megan went to get.

Two hours later, with a steaming-hot Thanksgiving dinner on the table, Jerod said grace. "Thank you, Lord, for the food set before us. I want to personally thank you for this past year. So many blessings this year, much more than I could have ever hoped for." He squeezed Dana's hand while everyone continued with their head bowed.

"Thank you for the hands that prepared this meal." Jerod paused when he heard a snort-laugh, then continued, "And thank you for those who will clean up the giant mess in the kitchen. They will earn today's feast, that's for sure."

All laughs stopped when the men, who all knew about the little food fight, realized they were the ones who would deserve the food.

"And I want to thank you for putting us all in a country that values their military and supports anyone who fights for the freedom we all hold so dear in this blessed land. I also want to ask that you change the hearts of those who would see our day of thanks end on a bad note. Please, Father, turn the hearts of those who wish to do harm today. Let America's families have one day to give thanks and enjoy time with you and their families. In Jesus' name we pray, amen."

All of the participants of the meal, including Dana and her family, echoed the amen as they raised their heads and smiled at

Jerod.

Megan knew that there were always going to be threats to her country. And holidays seemed to be bigger targets these days. But she also knew that worrying about what might happen wasn't worth it. She was glad to be in the company of all these heroes. She was going to enjoy today.

Tomorrow she would leave and deal with her mother, but today was about blessings and the family that Megan had chosen to be with.

Chapter 15

As per usual, Thanksgiving Day was a nice, quiet one around the Big Sky Christmas Tree Farm. Cody was feeling much better after his restful day yesterday, and today his grandfather had let him help with feeding the animals. That was the only chore anyone did on a big holiday.

Daniel and Uncle Steve spent the day stuffing themselves with the feast they all helped to prepare and they sat around the living room watching football games. It was the perfect bachelor's Thanksgiving.

Well, almost perfect.

An image of Megan standing in the kitchen cooking a giant turkey to perfection kept interrupting Daniel's thoughts. Even after they ate, he kept seeing her in a dress and apron. He wasn't sure what that was all about, as Megan didn't wear too many dresses.

Then when the football game started, he couldn't get the image of Megan out of his mind, so by half-time he stood up and walked to a back room and called the woman. He knew if he didn't speak with her, she'd stick in his mind and never leave him alone, just like a sticky candy cane stuck in a kid's head of hair all night after eating them in bed.

He'd know, since he'd done that once. But only once.

As a boy, he had taken a candy cane off the tree when no one was looking and snuck it in his bed for a late-night snack. Daniel was always getting hungry around midnight, and instead of getting something from the kitchen he started taking snacks to bed with him. That night, he'd unwrapped the candy cane and stuck it in his mouth. As he slept, the sugary stick made its way out of his mouth and into his hair. Little boys tend to squirm a lot in bed.

So when he woke up, it wasn't as though the midnight treat was just stuck to the side of his head. No, it was more like a string of Christmas lights had been woven through his head. Only these lights had the stripes of a candy cane and stuck to various parts of his head.

When he went downstairs, his uncle laughed and sat him down at the kitchen table before he cut the candy cane out of his hair and left a choppy look to his head. When the kids at school made fun of the chunks of missing hair, he decided never to eat candy in bed again. At least until he discovered Reese's Pieces didn't stick to one's head at night. Then he'd only have to take a shower to clean up if he fell asleep with candy in his hair.

Although showering as a young boy wasn't usually a fun experience, it was much better than the kids making fun of him for having chunks of hair missing thanks to a sticky candy cane that had woven its way all through his hair.

Daniel sat down on a chair in the back room and rubbed his sweaty palms down the sides of his jeans. He wasn't sure why he was so nervous, but he was. Even though it was perfectly normal for a guy to call his female friend on a major holiday and wish her a happy Thanksgiving. Didn't matter that he wanted more than friendship lately. Or did he? He was feeling confused all of sudden about what he wanted.

Or was it just the nerves? Megan was beautiful and sweet, she was always helping others, and they seemed to have a lot in common. Well, okay, maybe not a lot, but opposites attracted, right? At least that's what plenty of songs and poems said.

Why was this so difficult?

Daniel didn't even realize he'd hit the green dial button on his phone until he heard the ringing sound. Then he reeled in his thoughts and focused on the woman who answered the phone faster than he was prepared for.

"Daniel?" Megan's voice was tentative, sure, but there was also something else.

"Megan, happy Thanksgiving. I hope you had a wonderful meal today and the guys didn't stick all the cooking and the cleaning on you." He laughed imagining her in the kitchen right then and there in the dress and apron that had run through his mind earlier.

"Ah, thankfully the guys did the cleaning. But Dana and I did do all of the cooking. How was your Thanksgiving? Did you guys get a turkey and cook it yourself?" Her voice was still strained, but not as much as it had been when she answered.

He chuckled. "Yeah, it turns out Cody can cook a mean turkey. And the rest of us helped with some of the sides."

"Some of the sides?"

"Um, don't tell anyone, but last night I went and bought a few things that only needed to be heated up." Daniel grinned as he thought about the sides he'd bought premade from the local grocer.

"Like what?" Megan asked.

Daniel scratched his head. "Oh, like mashed potatoes, canned corn, rolls, and a few other items."

"So, what you're saying is you really only warmed up the side dishes? Did Cody actually cook a turkey, or did he just warm up a pre-cooked one?" When Megan laughed, Daniel knew she was relaxing and enjoying the conversation as much as he was.

"No, he did cook a turkey. It was raw when he bought it. But, um, yeah. That was really the only thing that was made from scratch."

They bantered back and forth for a few minutes until the line went silent. When Daniel thought maybe he had lost her, he asked, "Megan, you still there?"

She sighed. "Yeah. Sorry."

"What's wrong?" This time, he stayed silent until she spoke.

After what felt like hours, but was probably more like twenty seconds, Megan began to tell him what had been bothering her. "My mom is sick. I'm going to have to head out tomorrow and see her."

"I'm sorry. I hope it's nothing serious." He couldn't remember her ever saying much about her mom, so he didn't know if she was only dealing with a bad flu or if it was something worse, like cancer.

"I'm not exactly sure what's going on." Megan's voice broke.

All Daniel wanted to do right then and there was hold her in his arms tell her it was all going to be alright. But he couldn't. "Megan, I'll be right over."

"No, don't bother. I'll be fine. It's just bad timing." She inhaled. "That sounds awful, I know. But there's a history here."

"Do you have someone to talk to in person?" Daniel may not have been the best listener, but he would be there for her if she let him.

Megan took a moment, then sighed. "Not exactly. It's a house full of men. Mostly men I counsel."

"Is Dana still there?"

"She's with Jerod—they're going over wedding plans."

"I'm coming over, and I don't want any arguments." Daniel stood up and, still on the phone, walked out of the room.

"No, I'll be fine. Don't worry about me."

"I want to be there for you. Will you let me do that?"

A sniffle came over the phone, and Daniel knew he was doing the right thing.

<h1 style="text-align:center">Chapter 16</h1>

Megan was a strong woman. Shoot, she'd survived Afghanistan and was now working with servicemen who came home injured from war. Why couldn't she keep her emotions in check for one short phone call?

When she hung up the call with Daniel, she headed to her room to start packing. If Daniel was going to come over, she needed to get this done before he took up the rest of her evening. She hated to ruin the ending to everyone's Thanksgiving Day with her family drama. Her momma was sick, but it didn't mean anyone else had to worry about her. That was Megan's job.

While she packed, Megan prayed for her mom to get the help she needed. And to at least make it through the new year clean and sober. Only ten minutes into her packing, her phone rang. Thinking it was Daniel, she answered, "Change your mind already?"

"Sweetie?" The voice on the other end most certainly was not a sexy, masculine one.

"Mom? How are you?" Megan winced. Her mom was in the hospital; she couldn't be doing very well. "I mean, what's going on?"

"I'm fine. I just wanted to let you know that you don't need to come here. The doctors are going to release me tomorrow morning. Gus will come and get me."

"Wait, what?" Megan sat down hard on the edge of her bed. "I thought you had a heart attack?"

Her mom chuckled nervously. "So did I. Turns out it was just really bad indigestion. Probably from a bad turkey, or something else they served at the shelter last night."

"Why were you having dinner at a shelter?" Megan knew her mom was down on her luck, but she was supposed to be living in a special place for those receiving help for her issues. Kind of like a halfway house.

Silence.

Megan could hear her mom's shallow breathing, but she stayed quiet. Eventually, Megan knew what had happened. "You left, didn't you? Or you relapsed?"

"Oh, honey. That's not what happened."

Megan could picture her mother waving a dismissive hand and tsking away her questions. But she wasn't going to let the discomfort of discussing her mother's drug addiction stop her. "Mom, why did you leave your housing?"

"Because Gus came for me. You know how much I love him." Gus was her mother's on-again-off-again boyfriend and dealer. If Marianne Anderson was back with Gus, then she was also back on drugs.

"Mom, you aren't supposed to be with him, ever. He's not just a boyfriend, he's your dealer. You'll never get clean if you hang out with him or any of those so-called friends who keep giving you drugs." Frustration was building, and Megan was about to blow a gasket. How could someone be so stupid as to go back to a dealer when she had gotten clean?

Although, her mom had never been clean and sober for long. It wasn't surprising that she was off the wagon. It was one of the reasons Megan had left home the second she could.

Her experiences growing up had also given her knowledge that had helped her with her current career, and kept Megan away from drugs and alcohol her entire life. She never wanted to be like her mother, so she'd never even had a drop of alcohol in all her years, nor a taste of any drugs.

"Honey, don't worry. I'm clean. I swear it. I can't even remember the last time I did a line of coke. Honest."

Megan wasn't sure what to believe. She needed to go and see her mother. But she always got the creeps when Gus was around. "So, does this mean you don't want me to come visit?"

"Oh sweetie, I always want you to visit." Marianne coughed. "But you'll be more comfortable at a hotel than our apartment." They only had a one-bedroom apartment, which Megan would never even enter.

"If you're fine, then I'll wait a little bit. Maybe I'll come closer to Christmas to see you. And yes, I'll get a hotel room of my own." Megan shivered thinking about what their apartment must look like. She imagined rat infestations, roaches, spiders, and probably mold.

"Perfect. I'll be sure to get a Christmas tree this year." The perky notes in her mom's voice were almost enough to put a smile on Megan's face.

When they hung up, she did smile as she thought about Christmas trees. Oh, and Daniel. She should probably call him and tell him he didn't need to come by—her mom was going to be fine. Well, maybe not fine, but she was Marianne's version of normal.

As she hit the button on her phone to call Daniel, the doorbell rang. Of course.

"I'll get it," Megan called out as she headed to the front door knowing who it would be. "Daniel," she said as she opened the door.

The man standing on the porch had a worried look on his face. "Are you alright? I see you tried to call and then hung up."

She nodded. "Come in. I was going to tell you not to worry about stopping by, but you knocked as my phone started ringing."

He walked in and took off his hat.

Megan took his hat and coat and put them up on a peg by the front door. "Would you like some decaf coffee? Or hot cocoa?"

"Coffee would be wonderful, thanks." Daniel followed her into the kitchen, where she prepared him a mug of hot coffee. One of the best things about living on a ranch was the fact that they always had a hot, fresh pot of coffee going.

Once they were seated and sipping their hot coffee, Daniel began, "So, how's your mom?"

That was a loaded question if Megan had ever heard one. Or was her answer the loaded part? She took another sip of her coffee and held the cup in her hands. She didn't think she could look Daniel in the eyes, so she kept her gaze on her cup and noticed a tiny crack in the rim. It was one of her favorite mugs, too.

As Megan tried to get her head wrapped around what she was going to say, she noticed the logo on the mug and a tiny smile pulled at the corners of her mouth. The Big Sky Christmas logo and the red Christmas truck with a green tree sticking out of the bed brought her thoughts back to the tree farm, and Daniel. He was such a nice guy, even when he stuck his foot in his mouth.

But was she ready to dump her crazy family drama on him? Especially now that her mom wasn't in any more trouble than usual?

Daniel tilted his head and looked hard at Megan. "What's going on? First you seemed upset, and now you have a small smile."

With a heavy sigh, Megan went into the story about her mom leaving the hospital. She had decided he didn't need to know all the family drama. Maybe one day she would tell him what a rotten childhood she'd had, but not today. Today would be all about getting past her mom as quickly as possible. Then maybe they could talk about the tree farm.

"So, how are the calendar sales doing?" Even though Megan had heard from Sadie about how the sales were going, she thought it might be nice to turn the topic to something safe. And she was curious how the farm was faring. Everyone knew that the tree farm had been in trouble just a couple of months ago.

Daniel chuckled. "That calendar is a lot more popular than I could have ever imagined."

"Wishing you would have posed for it now?" Megan teased.

He shook his head. "No way. I'm even happier now that it's doing so well."

Jerod walked in and snorted. "You were smart. I can't tell you how many women ogle me when I go into town now. And none of us even took our shirts off. Why are the women going so crazy?" He grabbed a clean mug out of the cupboard above the coffee maker and poured himself a cup of hot decaf.

A slow grin crossed Daniel's face, and he barely held back a chuckle. "I also heard your ranch was decorated quite nicely with images of you."

Megan had no qualms about laughing; she let loose a cleansing laugh. "You should have seen this place. I'd swear the guys went to the printer and bought pages upon pages of just Jerod's month. Then they put them up all over the place. It looked more like a woman's version of a pin-up wall in a mechanic's shop."

"Hey now, be careful or you just might find yourself on Santa's naughty list." Jerod narrowed his eyes and pursed his lips before taking a sip of his coffee.

Megan held up her hands. "I don't think Santa is going to put me on the naughty list for the first time ever just for teasing you."

"Wait, you've never been on the naughty list?" Daniel asked incredulously.

She shook her head. "Nope."

"That doesn't surprise me." Jerod sighed. "She's the epitome of a goody-two-shoes. She probably never even peeked at her gifts under the tree when she was a kid."

Megan squirmed in her seat. Not because Jerod was right or wrong, but because she hadn't had a present under the tree since she was about five. Most of her childhood she didn't even have a tree. Growing up, the only Christmas presents she got came from her friends, or her best friend's mom. And only when she had been in one place long enough to make friends.

"Okay, enough about naughty lists. Something tells me that if I turn this back on you we'll find out you were never on the nice list." Megan smirked and pushed her childhood to the back of her mind.

Jerod turned to Daniel. "What about you, man?" He gave a quick nod. "Were you ever on the naughty list?"

Daniel chuckled and thought back to life in Frenchtown as a kid. "Living here with Santa Claus, it was rare anyone ever made the naughty list. When Santa's right here in your presence, you kinda need to be on your best behavior."

"Yeah, I can see that." Jerod took another sip of his coffee. "Growing up, we thought about Santa and his magical crystal ball. It seemed like something from a TV show, not real life."

"Ah, I see I was right." Megan chuckled. "You never made the nice list."

Jerod held up his hands. "Hey now, I resemble that remark." He chuckled. "Actually, I did make the list quite a few times. I think I was only bad enough to have my mom tell me I was on

Santa's naughty list once. Although, I still got presents that year. Just not the Game Boy I wanted." He shrugged.

Game Boy? Megan had never even thought of having one. When her friends had them she played theirs, but she knew her mom would never have the money to get her one. And if for some strange reason someone else would have bought her one, Megan's mom would have found it and pawned it when she needed money for drugs or booze. Megan never had anything nice or valuable for that very reason.

"It must have been nice growing up here so close to Santa." A feeling of longing, and maybe even pain, passed through Megan's heart. But she'd never hold it against anyone if they had a good childhood. She was actually happy to hear people talk about their happy lives. It helped her to know that there were still good families out there. Not everyone had grown up with heartbreak.

Daniel had a wistful look on his face as he gazed out the back kitchen window at the barn. "Yeah, it was really good. Even though my mom was single my entire childhood, we still had a pretty good life here. My Uncle Steve was really good about taking care of us both. And with our own Santa Claus, well"—he shrugged— "everyone had presents, no matter their situation."

Megan bit her tongue before she let on how rough her Christmases were. "I'm glad Frenchtown is so tight-knit."

Jerod shook his head. "No way. Everyone knows everyone else's business here. I don't like it."

Daniel laughed. "That's only because you can't walk down the street without the women gawking at you. Once the calendar is no longer new, you'll go back to being just one of us."

"I don't know about that." Jerod eyed Daniel warily. "I have a feeling I'll never be considered one of *us*."

Megan nodded. "He's right. You grew up here, Daniel, but we're new."

The trio spent the next few minutes discussing how small towns treat newcomers, and finally Jerod yawned and stretched his arms above his head. "Okay, okay. Tomorrow morning is gonna come early. I've gotta hit the hay. Good night y'all." He stood up and left to head to bed.

"He's right." Megan stood up, took her empty coffee mug to the sink, rinsed it out, and put it in the dishwasher next to Jerod's.

When Daniel took his to the sink, Megan took it from him and rinsed it out before adding it to the top rack. "Thank you," he said. "Will you tell me how your mom's doing later after you talk to her?"

Megan smiled. "Of course. And thank you again for coming over. I know you've got to be tired."

"It wasn't that long of a day. We sat around eating and watching TV most of the day. But Jerod was right, tomorrow morning is gonna come early." Daniel moved toward the front door, and Megan followed. "Will I see you out at the tree farm tomorrow?"

She opened the door for Daniel as he put his coat on. "Yes, I'll be bringing the guys over again. I'll come look for you when we get there."

Daniel smiled and put a hand on her arm. "I'll keep an eye out for you. Happy Thanksgiving, and I hope you get a good night's sleep."

Pink tinged her cheeks. "Thanks. You too."

Chapter 17

B lack Friday was always busy at the tree farm, and at the tree lot in town. Usually Daniel was swamped with ensuring there were plenty of trees cut and ready for those who didn't want to choose and cut their own.

This Black Friday was busy, but it was different.

With the carnival, the food booths, and the craft booths all set up and fully manned, the tree farm was busier than Daniel could ever remember it being in November. The first weekend of December was always the prime tree day, so both the lot and farm were swamped that weekend. But this year you'd think it was already December, and not November, with all of the customers on the farm.

"When did getting a Christmas tree trump the crazy Christmas shopping in stores?" Daniel asked Megan after they greeted one another.

She laughed. "Oh, Daniel. Have you ever heard of all-night sales?"

He furrowed his brow. "What?"

"Most of the Christmas shoppers have already done the bulk of their shopping today." She looked at her watch. "It's almost eleven in the morning and most early bird sales are done. People tend to shop online a lot more than they used to. Plus, most of the stores were open last night and never closed. Christmas shopping starts on Thanksgiving night now.”

With a shake of his head, Daniel scoffed. “What has this world come to?”

“Now you’re starting to sound like a curmudgeonly old man.” Megan arched a brow and pinched her lips in an effort to keep from laughing at the cute cowboy.

Daniel’s head shook back and forth so hard, he almost lost his hat. “Oh, no you don’t. I’m not old.”

“I never said you were. I only said you’re *acting like an old man.*”

“Well”—Daniel quirked his lips to the side—“I do spend a lot of time with a couple of old men.” He looked over Megan’s shoulder. “Speaking of which…”

Megan turned around and smiled when she caught sight of Joseph Makinaw walking with Santa. “Merry Christmas.” Since it was officially the start of the Christmas season, Megan was going to greet everyone with her preferred saying.

“Merry Christmas, Megan.” Santa grinned at her, then at Daniel. “Today looks to be a banner day, doesn’t it?”

The four of them spent some time on small talk, and then when the two older men walked away, Daniel grinned.

Megan narrowed her eyes. “I recognize the glint in your eyes.” She pointed at his face. “What’s going on with this?”

“I have a surprise for you.” Daniel took Megan’s hand and walked her to the other side of the barn.

“Just in time. Here ya go.” Javier handed the reins to Daniel, tipped his hat to Megan, and walked away without a backward glance.

Megan’s eyes widened. “I thought you’d need this for the crowds today?”

He shook his head. “Nope, not today. When it’s this crowded we can’t do sleigh rides. Too many people out and about on the farm. But we do have one sleigh for Santa to sit on and take pictures with the kids. This one"—he pointed to the one in front of them—"is for our use today."

"But, but…" She was tongue-tied. Daniel was so busy; how could he take her out?

"I can see the question in your eyes." Daniel stared into her eyes and took a step closer while holding the horse's reins in one hand. "I have to go out to one section of the ranch on business, but there's no reason why you can't join me for a ride on the sleigh, now is there?"

Megan tilted her head and looked up at him through her lashes. "I guess not."

Unbeknownst to them, the Claus couple were watching from where they stood taking pictures with the visiting families.

Mrs. Claus tapped her husband's shoulder. "See, Santa. I was right about them."

Santa followed his wife's gaze and watched the hesitant expression on Megan's face. "I don't know, my dear. You might have bitten off more than you can chew this year."

"Oh, pish." Jessica Claus waved a white-gloved hand in front of her face. "Those two go together like candy canes and ice cream."

"Ho, ho, ho. That's my favorite ice cream. But I don't know— this *couple* doesn't look so much like a couple, but more like a disaster waiting to happen." Santa's belly-full-of-jelly laugh brought a lot attention to him and his wife. So they turned their attention back to the families wanting to greet them and take pictures.

Once Megan and Daniel were both seated on the smaller sleigh, Daniel guided the horse slowly out and around the crowds. He did have to go and check on the larger trees in the back. They had received a call from the mayor of Bozeman; they needed another twenty-five-foot tree for a last-minute display in the mall.

Daniel knew that if he let himself enjoy the warmth of Megan sitting so close to him on the sleigh, he'd end up with his foot in his mouth again. Instead, he tried something different. Something his uncle had said the night before when they were talking about his foot-in-mouth disease.

"The news report has really helped our farm out, a lot. I can't believe all the people who've come looking for a real tree this year. And how far away they've come from." Daniel stopped the sleigh as a family of five who weren't paying any attention to their surroundings walked directly in front of them, looking with wide eyes at all the tall trees.

"Momma, I want that one." A little girl with blond pigtails pointed to one of the few fifteen-foot trees they had cut the night before and set close to the front for people to buy.

Megan grinned. "Do you think her parents will get her a tree that big?"

"I doubt it." Daniel shook his head. "They'd need one of those two-story living rooms. The kind with the windows that look out to an incredible view. Otherwise, the tree won't fit."

"You mean one of those houses with a wall of windows on one side, and the inside looks more like a mall or city center?" Megan chortled.

"That's it. Cathedral ceilings and all that. Yeehaw." Daniel urged the horses on once the family had cleared their path.

They made their way to the very back of the farm, and as they rode along they both enjoyed the companionable silence. Daniel wanted to say something, but he kept going back to his "medical" issue. He didn't want to offend Megan, not again. So he focused on making sure he didn't run anyone down, and they traveled slowly to the back lot of blue spruce trees.

"You said the mall wanted another tree?" Megan turned in her seat to look at Daniel when they were close enough to see the section of trees Daniel was aiming for.

"Yeah. I don't know why they wanted another tree—they already have a thirty-foot tree selected and tagged. It will go to them on Monday, when we're slower and they are as well."

"Cyber Monday usually does clear out the malls. That's a great time to put up a tree," Megan agreed.

Again, they conversation paused. Daniel wracked his brain to find something business-related they could talk about. In the past two days he had realized when he spoke business to Megan, he kept his boot out of his mouth. While he wanted to get to know her better, he decided to take it slow. Maybe once he felt more comfortable with her the conversation could become more personal. And he'd keep from showing his disease. One could hope.

Daniel brought the horse and sleigh to a halt when they were right next to the largest of the trees in that section. He stepped out and went around to tie the horse to a tree before moving to help Megan out of the sleigh. But by the time he got to her, she was already down on the ground and looking at the largest of the trees.

"How do you tell how tall they are? The mall asked for a specific height, didn't they?"

Trees. Daniel could talk trees until the reindeer came home. Anything to do with Christmas was comfortable and easy for him. "We have a few measuring sticks. But for the most part, I just eyeball the tree. I've been doing this for so long now that I just know about how tall a tree is."

"Really?" Her brows rose and she stopped in her tracks. "How tall is this one?" Megan pointed to the tree next to her, which towered above her.

It didn't take long for Daniel to come up with a number. "It's about ten feet, five inches, give or take a few inches." He walked over to where they kept one of the larger measuring rods and stood it up next to the tree. "Okay, back up until you have a good view of the top of the tree and the numbers on the rod." Daniel motioned for her to move back a couple more steps.

"Ah, it looks like it's about…" Megan tilted her head and squinted her eyes. Then she pursed her lips and put her hands on her hips. "You've measured this one before, haven't you?"

He pulled the rod away and set it up against one of the other trees. "Who? Me?" He pointed to himself. "Not that I can remember." One side of his mouth quirked up. "So, what's the height?"

"Ten feet, six inches." She glared at him.

Daniel put his hands up. "Alright, alright. I *might* have measured this one, or the one next to it, in the past couple of weeks." He chuckled. "But it was easy to guess. I know how tall you are, and when you stood next to the tree it wasn't difficult to see that it towered over you by close to three feet."

"I'd say it's exactly three feet taller than I am. Seeing as how I'm five feet, six inches tall."

"Come on, we've got to find a taller tree." Daniel waved her on as he hid his smile. Things were mostly about business, but he was getting a little bit of personal info on her as they went. Maybe this was how he needed to go—very slow and keep things less personal? At least until he was more comfortable and could speak without eating his own feet.

It didn't take long for Megan to find the perfect tree for the mall's second display. "Here, this is the one. It looks like it would be at least twenty-five feet tall." She waved her hand in front of a beautiful, tall, and very full blue spruce.

Without a word, Daniel walked around it slowly, inspecting the tree for large spots or any areas that might be dying. It was rare, but sometimes larger trees like this had sections where the needles had started to turn brown. It had to do with water distribution among the trunk and branches. If there wasn't enough water during the years, the tree tended to focus on ensuring most of it thrived by cutting water off from some parts. It was almost like the trunk and branches were part of a conscious being, and some parts would sacrifice themselves for the greater good.

"This is a beautiful specimen. And I think you're right, it's going to be very close to the target height." Daniel looked around for a pole tall enough to measure the tree in question. When he found one marked thirty feet, he carried it over to the tree.

"Yup, you guessed it." Daniel grinned as he held the extremely tall pole with both hands and looked between the rod and the tree. "But can you do me a favor and step back a little bit and get a more accurate reading?" From his spot next to the tree, it was difficult to see exactly how the top tip of the tree measured.

Megan took several steps back. She angled her head a few different ways and walked away and then forward a couple times. Eventually, when she was satisfied, she took three steps closer and gave Daniel a thumbs-up. "I'd say it was just about perfect. It's only two inches shorter than the requested twenty-five feet."

"Good job, Megan." Daniel set the pole down on the ground and turned back to the beautiful woman. "You know, if you ever lose interest in working on a ranch you can always come here and work on a tree farm instead." It took everything he had to keep from winking at her. Something inside of him must have been broken, since he was constantly wanting to wink at the pretty little lady.

"Thanks, I'll keep that in mind if the whole counseling thing doesn't work out for me." Megan rolled her eyes and watched Daniel as he tagged the tree for the Bozeman mall.

Chapter 18

It was touch and go there for a moment, but Megan couldn't believe that Daniel had kept the conversation either on business or lighthearted banter. He didn't once make her cringe with stupid comments. They were making strides in their friendship.

That was all it was, of course. They hadn't known each other long, and Megan wasn't the least bit interested in a relationship. No matter how cute the ginger-haired cowboy was.

Or how sweet he was when dealing with little old ladies.

Or how helpful when dealing with families.

No, stop it, she chided herself. Now wasn't the time to let her head fill with visions of sugar plums and handsome cowboys. She still had a lot of work to do on the ranch. They needed to secure more funding. And she still hadn't found a way to reach Sam. Could she arrange for three ghosts to visit him? Sam wasn't exactly a scrooge; he could be generous when he wanted. But he didn't have the Christmas spirit in him.

While driving everyone home that day, she thought about Sam and how he seemed to wear a permanent scowl on his face all day long. It seemed the closer they got to Christmas, the worse Sam got.

When she exited the truck back at the Crooked Arrow, she asked the guys, "Who's up for going into town tomorrow night for their annual Thanksgiving dinner?" Megan rubbed her hands together in anticipation of the famous pumpkin pies she'd heard so much about.

As expected, everyone but Sam raised their hand.

Jerod walked outside at the same time and narrowed his eyes at Sam when the guy only scowled at Megan. He put a hand on the man's shoulder. "Sam, it looks like everyone wants to attend the famous local dinner tomorrow. What's wrong?"

"I don't like crowds." Sam turned to leave, but Jerod stopped him.

"Then why do you keep volunteering at the tree farm? From what I've seen, there's so many more people there."

"That's exactly why I don't want to go. Too many people lately." Sam harrumphed and then headed inside without waiting for anyone to comment or follow him.

Once they were alone, Megan asked Jerod about Sam's story. "He hasn't told me much. At least not much more than what was in his file from the VA. Do you know why he's so unhappy?"

Jerod rubbed the scruff on his chin. Since Megan had been spending her days at the tree farm with most of the guys, he'd had to take up the slack and tend to the animals in addition to fixing anything that needed it. The ranch had been old and falling into disrepair when he'd bought it. So yeah, there were a lot of things still to fix. "I don't really know anything more than you."

"But you have some suspicions?" Megan tilted her head and considered her boss. Since coming to Crooked Arrow, they had gotten closer. Not in a romantic way—he was engaged to a wonderful woman, after all. But they had become so much more than just employee and employer. They were becoming friends.

"I don't think it's my place to say anything. At least, not yet. Give him some time to come to know you and feel comfortable with you. I'm sure he'll eventually open up. For some men it just takes a bit more patience." Jerod nodded at Megan and joined the others inside for a cup of pipin'-hot coffee and a slice of huckleberry pie.

One of the things she liked so much about Jerod was the fact that he didn't gossip. Instead of trying to pry the information out of her boss, Megan followed him inside and enjoyed the treat with everyone else. Even Sam was there.

"This is some good pie," Sam said before taking the last bite.

Megan sat back in her chair and began to feel a bit better about everything. Sam had found something he liked, and even commented on it. Maybe he needed to help out more in the kitchen? Could it be he enjoyed cooking, or baking? With all of the upcoming potlucks and dinners, Megan just might find a way to break through Sam's defenses.

The next day was hectic, but fun. All of the guests at the Crooked Arrow were so excited about the town's annual Thanksgiving potluck that they did their chores as quickly as they could so they could all get in a good shower. Some really needed it, too.

Dana had come by after her shift at the Frenchtown Roasting Company to help Megan make a few pies to bring. Megan wasn't the best baker, but she had found a few recipes over the years that she liked. One being apple streusel crumble. It wasn't exactly a pie—it was more like someone made a pie and it fell apart so they poured it into a casserole dish and topped it with yummy caramel apple streusel. They made three for the big shindig that night before Megan got ready herself.

Since Thursday, Megan had left two messages for her mom. She wanted to see how her mother was getting along since being released from the hospital. And if it really was only a bad turkey.

But her mom hadn't answered her cell phone or returned any messages. However, she decided to try once more.

"Hi, Mom. It's Megan. I just wanted to call one more time to see how you are. Please let me know, will ya? I've gotta go, the town is having a huge community Thanksgiving supper tonight. We're all going. I'm bringing that apple streusel you liked so much." She sighed and said goodbye, hoping her mom would call back soon.

They had never been close, but Marianne was her mom. Maybe if she made more of an effort, her mom would be open to the specialized help she needed.

Megan and Daniel hadn't made actual plans to attend the dinner together, but she hoped she would see him there. And maybe a small part of her wanted him to sit next to her. It was childish and she knew it, but her heart wanted what it wanted. It was her head that was going to make sure they didn't get into any trouble.

Sadly, the moment she saw him her head went blank and her heart sped up to triple time. The man walked in wearing clean cowboy boots, black jeans that hugged in the right places, and a dark-blue western shirt. His Stetson was black and fit his head perfectly. He even had on a bolo tie with a turquoise slide. He was stunning.

Megan tried to lick her lips, but her mouth had gone dry and therefore her tongue was, too.

Dana walked up next to her. "Careful, girl. Someone might get the wrong impression about what's happening with you and Daniel." She giggled and handed Megan a cup of water. "Here, I think you need this more than I do."

The man in question hadn't noticed her yet, so she took a few quick sips just to wet her whistle. But when he did look her way, she almost dropped the cup.

Daniel saw her and his lips curved up in a sultry smile while the laugh lines around his eyes crinkled. Even his eyes lit up when he noticed her. A gleam Megan didn't recognize was shining, and she hoped it was all for her and not one of the other women in town looking to bag a cowboy this Christmas.

Only yesterday at the tree farm she'd heard two women discussing what they wanted to find under their Christmas tree that year, and both agreed that a cowboy all wrapped up with a pretty red ribbon was what they wanted. At the time, Megan had rolled her eyes. But if Daniel were waiting for her under her tree, she just might have to believe in Santa.

That thought brought her up short. Didn't she already believe? She'd seen enough so far with the town's Santa and Mrs. Claus to know that the tradition of Santa was alive and well in Frenchtown.

When Daniel drew near, she felt her heart pitter patter in her chest and she had to take a few breaths to make sure it didn't beat so hard that Daniel would see it.

He took her hands and looked her up and down appreciatively. "Megan, you look"—he took a deep breath and seemed to stop himself from saying something before continuing—"beautiful. Can I say you take my breath away?"

All this time of him putting his foot in his mouth or doing that stupid winking thing, and he'd finally got it right. She sighed and felt her face relax before she smiled shyly. "Thank you, Daniel. You look very handsome yourself."

"I'd say you two look the perfect picture." Mrs. Claus beamed. "Speaking of which, have you had your pictures taken with Santa yet?"

Feeling a bit nervous, Megan answered, "No, ma'am. Not yet."

"Well, tonight is the perfect night. You both look so good. Why don't you go sit on Santa's lap and get your pictures taken

—together." Mrs. Claus nodded toward her husband and arched a brow when the couple stood there, letting their cheeks turn pink.

Megan couldn't remember when she'd last taken a picture with Santa. Whenever it was, the photo was long gone. Lost in one of the many moves they'd made when she was younger. Which might account for the boxes of mementos she'd kept from her years in the Army.

The thought of taking one now, well, it excited her. Was it because it was with Daniel? Or did she like the idea of having a picture with Santa that she could carry around with her forever? If she was being honest with herself, it was probably a bit of both. Maybe even a tad bit more to do with Daniel than she was ready to admit.

Not thinking, Daniel put his hand out for Megan and she took it. His soft smile sent her stomach tumbling around like a dryer on high speed. The feel of his work-rough hand in hers was oddly satisfying. The calluses that he'd developed working at the tree farm rubbed against her soft hands.

There was something masculine about a rough hand in hers. It made her feel like she was with someone who could protect her. Megan knew plenty of men with softer hands who could do a lot of damage to an enemy, but this particular hand in hers left her feeling safe. Something she really hadn't felt in a long time, if ever.

Most girls grew up with a father to protect them, or at least make them feel protected. But Megan had never known her father. Her mother had never even told her his name. And the string of men her mom had dated were more apt to hurt Megan than protect her, so she really wasn't sure what to do with these new emotions.

Was this protection she was feeling? Or did she just crave this feeling so much that she'd turned this new emotion into what she wanted? All she knew was that it was a new feeling and she craved more of it. Needed more of it. Megan squeezed Daniel's hand lightly, and he returned the gesture and smiled at her.

"What do you say we go get our picture with Santa?" he asked.

"As long as I can also tell him what I want for Christmas." Megan giggled. She actually giggled like one of those young girls she'd seen all over social media. Who was she and what had happened to her?

"I like it when you laugh. It softens your features and… I don't know…" He put his other hand on his stomach. "It does something exciting to me." Daniel looked down at his boots.

Megan noticed his red cheeks and felt hers burning as well. "I like it when you laugh as well."

They both stopped in the path of others and stood there staring at each other like love-sick puppies. It didn't last long, though.

"Hey, move it along. You're blocking the path." Sam looked between them. "If you want to stare into each other's eyes like teenagers, then go out back like the rest." He gestured with his thumb over his shoulder in the direction of the back door. Then mumbled under his breath, "Geesh, you'd think two grown adults would know better." The grumpy old man walked around them, shaking his head.

The rude interruption shattered the little bubble the couple had been in.

"Um, well. I guess we should go get in line." Megan bit her lower lip and looked toward the line for Santa.

"Yeah, we don't want to cause a traffic jam in here."

"If you aren't careful," Mike Blankenship interjected, "you might get pie in the face. And no one wants this aromatic pie to be wasted." He pointed to the table closest to them covered in all sorts of pies.

It was enough to break the tension that had crept up between Megan and Daniel. Both laughed and moved on.

"You know, I can't get a beat on that Mike character." Daniel, still holding Megan's hand, looked thoughtfully back at the big guy.

"Until recently I thought he was an extreme introvert who only talked about his cows. But since we've been helping out at the tree farm, he's evolved." Megan wanted to say more, but patient confidentiality caused her to stop.

Her studies had taught her that getting the men to do work or chores that they liked would help, but Mike had been working with the cows for months and stayed inside his protective walls. She looked back at him and noticed he was smiling and waving at some of the people she'd seen at the tree farm lately. She needed to talk to Jerod about what she'd seen in all of the men since helping out at the tree farm. Other than Sam, all of them had made positive changes.

Could it be the tree farm held some sort of magical medicine, or was it just the magic of the Christmas season bringing out the joy in her patients? There was something about the farm that got to her, too.

Or was it Daniel?

Chapter 19

S unday morning came early, and Daniel was ready to get up and greet the day with a smile. The town's annual Thanksgiving dinner had gone so much better than he could have hoped, and he had a souvenir to remember it always. The picture of him and Megan was sitting on his dresser. As soon as he got the chance, he was going to get a frame for it and put it up on the wall.

It was the first night he hadn't made her scowl at him, and he wanted to remember that night forever. Hopefully it was a sign that he was learning how to speak to women, especially Megan.

Cody walked past him as they worked to get the tree farm ready to open. He stopped and glared at Daniel. "All morning now you've had this crazy grin on your face, even while we watched the church service. What's got you so happy?" Light dawned, and he held his hands up before Daniel could answer. "Wait, this is about last night, isn't it? I saw you and Megan holding hands and getting a picture taken with Santa." Then he frowned. "But I thought she despised you?"

"That was what I thought, too. Maybe all those sleigh rides helped to soften her up to my charms?" Daniel rubbed his knuckles on the outside of his jacket, over his chest.

Cody pushed his friend, hard.

Daniel fell into a pile of snow they had just blown to the side of the walkway.

"Hey, what's that for?" Daniel got up and brushed the slushy white stuff from his pants and glared when he felt the cold wet seeping into his jeans.

"That, my good friend, is what happens when you stop paying attention to your work and daydream about a pretty cowgirl."

Daniel grinned and barreled into his friend, knocking them both into a pile of wet, slushy snow.

"Hey, I wasn't the one who was daydreaming about a pretty girl," Cody complained.

"Yes, but I deserved a little retribution. Especially after all the times I've caught you daydreaming about a particular brunette lately." Daniel arched a knowing brow and nodded toward the gate where said brunette was standing, laughing.

"What in tarnation has caused the two of you to try and become snowmen?" Sadie laughed and shook her head, keeping a safe distance from the rascals.

Both men scrambled to their feet and began rigorously cleaning the snow off their clothes.

"Sorry about that." Daniel gave Sadie a sheepish grin.

Cody laughed. "Just two strong rancher sorts getting a bit of fun in. That's all."

Sadie crossed her arms over her chest and pursed her lips. "Mm-hm. I bet. You better change before you catch your death of cold." Then she motioned for them to go inside. As she sashayed away, she mumbled, "Boys."

Daniel put his arm around Cody's shoulder. "So, how goes that?" He motioned with his eyes toward Sadie. Cody and Sadie had been spending a lot of time together lately and everyone knew they'd end up together, maybe even get married. Recently they'd had their first date, although it didn't end too well when they were almost run over by a car and Cody's own truck. But both had come through fine and were almost healed.

"Probably better than you and Megan." Cody grinned and ran into the house before Daniel could tackle them to the snow once more.

If Daniel thought he was going to have a smooth afternoon, he was sorely mistaken. There seemed to be trouble after trouble all day. He should have expected issues when they had that many people on the farm.

Diego, one of the carnies, walked up to Daniel looking frazzled. "Man, I don't know if we can keep this up. We've run out of food again. And I don't know if my supplier can increase our order any more than they already have."

Daniel wiped a hand down his face. This wasn't the first person to say they were running out of food. If only they'd planned better. If this kept up, they'd have to slaughter a neighbor's cow just to keep beef going. And they'd need at least a hundred more chickens.

Well, now Daniel felt a lightbulb turning on above his head. "I don't know how to help with veggies or grains, but I think I might know someone who can help with meat."

"I'd take any help I can get. We can always change up our menus to accommodate stews, or..." Diego rubbed the scruff on his chin. "Maybe we could do something around gluten-free menus? To help ration the rest of our breads. You know, like bunless burgers, soups with no bread. That sort of thing."

"Yeah, that could help. But we might be able to get some more breads. Let me call my friends and see what they can do. How would bison burgers go over?"

Diego's eyes bulged. "Well, they do tend to have ground beef mixed in with the bison, but yeah. That would go over very well with most of these people. Bunless, too."

"Okay, I'll get back to you later today. I know a few ranchers who might be able to sell us a few head of their cattle." As Daniel walked away from Diego, he called up Matthew Manning from the Triple J Ranch over in Beacon Creek. Chloe Manning, now Chloe Beck, had moved to town just over two years ago and he'd met her brother when he came to town for her wedding to Brandon Beck. They'd struck up a friendship and had chatted a few times.

"Matthew, howdy." Daniel grinned while he chatted with his new friend.

"Hey Daniel, how goes it? I hear you're selling trees by the ton." Matthew chuckled.

"Yeah, about that." Then Daniel went into the story of how many customers they'd had recently and how all of the food vendors were running short on beef and chicken, along with everything else.

"Well, I can't help you with the chicken, but I can help with beef. I also have a buddy in Montana who raises bison. They might be able to help. And one of our neighbors raises pigs."

"All of it, please." Things were starting to look up for Daniel. The rest of the problems were more about competing moms wanting the same tree or kids running around like little madmen. Although, at right about five o'clock he did come upon a little girl crying. She was maybe six years old and had a completely red face covered in tears and mucus. She was running in circles just bawling.

Daniel ran to the little girl and leaned down on one knee just as a grandmother type did the same. "Oh, sweetie. Please don't cry." Daniel's heart strings were being pulled like he'd never felt before. He'd dealt with plenty of crying kids over the years, but none of them had affected him like this little girl.

"Hunny, where's your momma?" the grandmotherly woman asked.

The girl didn't answer. Instead, she ran right into Daniel's arms and wrapped her tiny little arms around his torso. Her hands barely made it past his sides.

"Oh darlin', I'm so sorry. How can Uncle Daniel help?" He wasn't her uncle, but the little girl had taken a liking to him, so he'd play the part. But when his nose began to burn and his eyes watered, he wondered who he was and where his masculinity had run to. He'd never cried over a lost little girl before. Without even realizing it, he had wrapped his arms around the little girl with brown pigtails and a pink unicorn parka. When he stood up, he looked around hoping to find a frantic mother or father. All he saw were people gawking and the grandmotherly woman wiping tears from her own eyes.

"Is she yours?" the elderly matron asked.

"No, ma'am. I've never seen her before. Do you know her?"

The woman shook her head. "She's sure taken a shining to you, though."

Daniel patted the girl's back and whispered, "What's your name, sweetie?"

"Manda." The little girl hiccuped and went back to crying, but it was much softer this time.

Daniel hoped and prayed that she'd stop crying soon. He needed to get his walkie out and ask if anyone had seen a set of parents missing a little girl.

When his walkie squawked, he tried to hand the girl to the grandmother. "Can you hold her?"

"Sure thing, dear." The older lady tried to take the little girl from Daniel, but she was holding onto his neck now with all her strength.

"Nooo, I want my Uncle Daniel!" she screamed, looking like she was about to turn the waterworks on again.

"Shh, it's alright. I've got you, darlin'." Daniel held the girl tighter to his chest and gave the older lady an apologetic look.

"Say, could you get the walkie-talkie off my belt and see what they want?"

"Sure thing." The lady took the walkie and pushed the button. "Grandma Sweets here, we've got a 10-65. She's about five with brown pigtails and a pink unicorn parka. Over."

Daniel raised his brows and stared at the woman who sounded like a police dispatcher.

She grinned. "What? I used to drive a truck with my husband. Long haul."

Daniel chuckled and felt the little girl move her head on his chest and look up at him. "Of course."

"Who's Grandma Sweets? Does she have candy?" Manda's face was beginning to clear up and it appeared as though she had wiped every bit of her tears, and other, uh, stuff on Daniel's chest.

He gulped and realized he'd need a clean jacket once he helped the little girl find her parents.

Grandma Sweets was going back and forth on the radio with Javier about the little girl, so he felt confident they'd find her parents.

"I don't think she has candy. But I know someone who does." Daniel looked out over the crowd, trying to find just the right person.

A tiny smile was his reward. "Who?"

When Daniel spotted the person he wanted, he looked down at Manda and said, "Santa Claus." Then he nodded toward the jolly ol' elf himself.

"Santa!" Manda screamed out and tried to wiggle out of his arms. But Daniel held tight. This was probably how Manda had lost her parents to begin with, and he wasn't about to lose this precious little girl before he could reunite her with her parents.

Chapter 20

When all the commotion about a crying girl made its way to Megan's ears, she hurried up and went to find the poor thing. She should have known the girl would be alright. But what surprised her was how tender Daniel was with the little tyke. And the girl, you'd think she thought he was her daddy or something with the way she clung to him.

Megan had to wonder if the girl knew Daniel from somewhere. Since he had it all under control, she stayed back and watched. Something inside of her needed to know how this would end, but something else—her heart maybe?—needed to know how Daniel would handle it all. She had to chide herself for judging him on how he took care of the crying girl. It shouldn't matter to her. All that mattered was that the girl was safe and they found her parents.

Which they did.

As Megan watched, her heart swelled with pride, or was it admiration? That cowboy was something else. He may have trouble speaking to women, but he was as comfortable with little girls as he was with Christmas trees.

When the parents showed up, they were both crying. And oh so grateful to Daniel and the old lady who talked on the radio like she was a trucker, or a cop. The little girl, however, was too busy licking the candy cane Santa had given her to even notice that her parents had arrived. Once she was done telling Santa what she wanted, she turned to her mom and dad and held her arms out.

Both parents hugged her tight. When they walked away, Megan noticed Daniel watching them with a wistful look on his face. It was almost as though he was wishing for a little girl of his own.

She took a closer look at the girl as they walked by her and she smiled to herself. The little girl reminded her of herself when she was that age. Megan didn't have many photos of herself as a kid, but her grandmother had left her a photo album with plenty of pictures of her when she was in first and second grade.

As a little girl, she too preferred to wear her brown hair in pigtails with pink ribbons. While she didn't have a pink unicorn parka, she did have a pink zippered hoodie that she remembered carrying around with her everywhere she went. Even in the summer.

A feeling of contentment and joy filled her as she remembered the good times she had spent with her grandmother before she passed away. Her grandmother would have loved this tree farm, and the craft fair.

"Hey, there you are. Did you hear what just happened?" Daniel walked up to Megan and gave her a quick hug.

The hug came from nowhere, and Megan took a step back.

"Sorry, too soon for friendly hugs?" He gritted his teeth, praying he hadn't stepped in it again.

"Well, no. But you might want to change your jacket before hugging anyone else." Megan pointed to the slimy goo running down the front of his coat.

He looked down. "Ah, yes. That would be Manda's doing." Daniel chuckled. "I'll have to see if I have an extra jacket here."

"Well, if it doesn't come out, it was well worth the loss. I saw how she clung to you. Very sweet." It was Megan's turn to surprise him when she winked at him.

Daniel was shocked into silence. Then he chuckled. "Well, I'll be…"

Before he could say anything else, Megan's phone rang. She pulled it out of her jacket pocket and motioned that she needed to get it.

He waved and headed toward the house.

Megan watched him walk away as she answered her phone. "Hey, Mom." She was a little surprised to be hearing from her mother so soon; it had only been two days since their last conversation. If she spoke to her mother more than once a month, it was surprising.

When the person on the other end of the phone spoke, she stood up straight and her mouth went dry. It wasn't her mother calling her, even though the caller ID said it was.

Megan had to sit down. The news wasn't good. She had just hung up the phone when Daniel found her.

"See, I got a clean jacket. How about…" Daniel leaned over and looked into Megan's ashen face. "What's wrong?" He took the seat next to her and held her in his arms as she took her turn crying into his chest.

While she let her tears flow, Daniel stayed quiet. He held her and rubbed her back. He was actually really good at this. He didn't even try to tell her all would be fine or ask her what was going on. At least not after that first time.

Megan pulled on the front of his jacket and wiped her nose. Something in the back of her mind reminded her that she had tissue in her pockets, and cleaning her snot on a man's jacket wasn't exactly lady-like.

When she had gotten herself under control, she pulled back just enough to look into his eyes. "I'm so sorry. I know you just had to change jackets because a little girl cried into your chest. You probably don't have another clean one here."

"Shh, it's alright. Don't worry about it. I can always steal one of Cody's. He won't mind." Daniel ran a hand down her arms and waited for her to tell him what had happened.

"It's my mom. She's been arrested."

Daniel's mouth opened and closed like a fish out of water.

Megan snorted. "Yeah, I've got a jailbird for a mother. This isn't the first time." She pulled back, and Daniel took her hands.

They stood there silent for a few moments, and Daniel scuffed his toe on the snow in front of them.

Megan tried to let go of his hand, but he wouldn't let her. "Look, I know I'm not the best person to talk to, especially now, but if you want to talk I'll listen."

With a deep sigh, Megan nodded and began to tell her tale about her drug addicted mother. "She's why I joined the Army straight out of high school." She tilted her head. "Well, that and I needed money for college. I joined and got the Army college fund with a special kicker. They ended up paying for my entire undergraduate degree. So it made it easier to get a master's on my own dime. Which I only had to pay for about half of since I qualified for quite a few minor scholarships and grants."

When the silence was awkward, Daniel tried to speak but found he couldn't say anything meaningful. "Look, I want to say something, but I'm afraid it'll come out lame and maybe even offend you. I'm working on what comes out of my mouth, but I think I still have a ways to go. I'm so sorry. But—" Daniel weighed his words carefully before speaking.

Megan stayed quiet, looking down at their still entwined hands. She too was holding firm now and not letting go.

"I think you're one of the bravest people I've ever met. Growing up the way you did, I don't know how you can be so normal and healthy." He looked into her face, as serious as she'd ever seen him.

Megan scoffed. "Really? I'm no better than anyone else."

Daniel shook his head. "No, you're the one with her head on straight. You're the one who helps others in need. Look at all of those men at the ranch you help daily. I've seen a major improvement in most of them."

"Yeah, but what about Sam? I've not done anything to help him." She looked down at her feet and sighed.

"I think you've done more than you realize." Daniel put two fingers under her chin and tilted her head up to look at him. "Sure, he's difficult to deal with, but when he comes to work here now he actually works most of the time. When he started, well, I wasn't too happy about him being here. And I had to make sure he stayed away from the visitors. He was scary."

"What do mean 'was?'" A small smile teased the edges of her lips.

Daniel chuckled. "Alright, he still is. But you've done wonders with him. You're the healthiest person I've ever met. You can handle anything you set your mind to."

Megan ran her free hand over her face as tears began to fall. "Not always."

His head jerked back and his brows furrowed. "What does that mean?"

"Nothing." She shook her head.

"Come on, we're both doing really well here. Don't close up on me now. If the roles were reversed and one of your patients was standing here with you, what would want them to do?"

"I'd want them to keep talking. It's better to get it all out in the open and then deal with emotions." She took a shuddering breath.

Daniel stayed quiet as she pulled herself together, again.

"I was in Afghanistan, right out of AIT…"

"Wait, what's AIT?" It was obvious Daniel had tried to stay quiet, but the questioning look on his face made it clear he really was confused.

"Advanced Individual Training. It's where we learn our jobs. While we are all soldiers and learn how to march and take orders as well as shoot a gun during basic training, AIT is where we get individual training for a job. I was a truck driver. Very common job for women these days." She winced when an image of her life in Afghanistan flashed before her eyes.

Megan was very patriotic, always had been. When she was little and whatever town she lived in had a Fourth of July parade, she always lined up and waited to smile and wave at the military people. Even if her mom wasn't coherent she'd still go on her own, or with a friend when she had one.

Daniel sucked in his lips. It looked like he was about to speak again, but didn't.

"Anyways, I'd only been on the job a few months. I had just turned nineteen and thought I could do anything. I was sent out to escort a group of doctors and nurses who were inoculating the women and children in a tiny village. There were very few men there. Most of those who were there were old. It wasn't until later that I discovered the men, and even the young boys, were taken by a local militia to serve in their ranks. Not by choice, but by force. Very common. Only the old or infirmed were left behind to tend to the women and young children. Something must have gone wrong, or the insurgents didn't like that we were taking better care of those left behind than they were. So they decided to attack."

Daniel gasped and looked her up and down. "But you don't look like you were injured."

"I was lucky—most weren't. The worst of my injuries ended up being mental. I was medically discharged for PTSD. When I was going through counseling for what I experienced, that's when I knew what I wanted to do. So I went to college to be a counselor for returning vets." One lone tear ran down her cheek.

Daniel put his hand up to wipe the tear away. "You are unbelievably brave. And lucky."

She shook her head. "It wasn't luck or bravery. God protected me. He has a plan for my life. I think I had to go through that in order to be able to help the returned men and women who don't know the love of God to recover."

He pulled her tight to his chest and held her longer than she could have hoped for.

Megan's heart rate had jumped sky high as she told her story, but as Daniel held her, she relaxed and her heart returned to normal. Once she was ready to look him in the eye again, she pulled back and gave him a tentative smile. "Thanks. I think I needed that."

"Sweetheart, that was more for me than you. But I'm glad it helped you as well. I can't believe everything you've been through and how healthy you sound. God really did protect you, didn't He?"

Megan nodded. "Yeah, He did."

Chapter 21

Daniel still couldn't get Megan's story out of his head, and heart. He'd never met anyone, male or female, as strong and courageous as Megan. He doubted he'd ever meet anyone like her again.

How could someone who had experienced the horrors of war, and not even a conventional war, come home and decide to get the training she did so she could help others who had experienced even worse?

It was more than emotion that flared within him—it was a strong desire to protect, and even help, this young woman who had burrowed her way into his heart without him even knowing it. Daniel wasn't sure if Megan was ready for him, but until the time was right he'd be there as her friend. He would be the one she turned to when she needed a shoulder to cry on.

While his mother had dated men—no, scratch that; rats, she had never gotten into the sort of trouble that Megan's mom had—he couldn't imagine what life would have been like if his mother cared more about her next fix than putting dinner on the table for him. Sure, his uncle had helped them both out a lot while he was growing up, but that's what family does.

How could a mother want drugs and evil men more than she wanted to take care of her daughter? Was that why Megan was letting her mother sit in jail?

He recalled the rest of the conversation from last night.

"Megan, what are you going to do about your mother?" he had asked.

She sighed. "This might sound harsh, but I'm not going to do anything more than pray right now."

"What?" Incredulity filled his voice. Even though her mother was a piece of work, she didn't deserve to rot in jail. Did she?

Megan took his hand and held it in both of hers. "Daniel, I know you can't understand this, but there comes a point in time when you have to let someone you love hit rock bottom. I thought she had done that last time."

"Last time?" Daniel interrupted.

"This isn't the first time she's been arrested for drugs. About three years ago her boyfriend and drug dealer had her making his deliveries for him. She was caught, but he wasn't."

"And he didn't help her, did he?"

Megan shook her head. "No. He left her in jail. Didn't even help out with a lawyer. I was finishing my training and didn't have the money to help, so she got whatever guy the courts assigned to her. He wasn't bad, but most of those who do pro-bono work are just trying to get their hours in."

"She went to prison?"

"No, since it was her first offense for supposedly selling drugs, the judge remanded her to a sort of camp. It was a drug detox facility. They helped her to get clean and see the error of her ways. Then she went into a halfway house. She wasn't supposed to have anything to do with her ex, but when she went to the hospital on Thanksgiving…" Megan shrugged.

"He came back into her life?"

She rubbed her chin. "He probably never left her life."

"And now?" Daniel asked.

"And now?" Megan blew out a long breath. "I have to let her feel the punishment for what she's done. I learned in my classes that you can't make anyone give up on drugs. They have to get to a point where they want to let it go themselves. Most hardcore druggies have to experience prison before they'll give up that life. And some?" She pursed her lips. "Some never do. No matter what their family does for them."

The silence that ensued was enough to get Daniel thinking he had to help Megan. She had no family other than her mom—that she knew of, anyway. And here she was trying to do right by her mom as well as work hard to be there for the returning vets who needed her help. At least those guys really wanted to get better.

"Hey, get your head out of the clouds and help me, why don't ya?" Cody called out, waving to get Daniel's attention.

Daniel shook his head and tried to put aside the thoughts of what he'd learned the previous night. It was the Monday after Thanksgiving and they were going to be very busy today. It was the start of the big push for people to buy trees and take them home. Since they had pre-sold a ton, they'd probably have hundreds of people coming in to cut their trees and take them. At least he'd be busy and not have to keep thinking about Megan's mom.

What a horrible way to grow up. He was going to make sure she knew he cherished and cared for her. Daniel had no clue how Megan had come to know the Lord, but he was thankful she had given her life to God. While the good Lord never promised us a pain-free or easy life here on Earth, He did promise to take care of us. And thinking back on all of what Daniel had learned, he didn't doubt one bit that God had taken care of Megan and brought her here, to Frenchtown, in order to do something big.

Whatever happened between them, Daniel wanted to see—and help, if possible—what the Lord would do through Megan

Anderson. For he knew without a shadow of a doubt it was going to be glorious.

It wasn't an hour later that Daniel was laughing and joking around with some of the local teens as they had a snowball fight, away from the other customers. Sometimes a kid just needed to blow off some steam.

And sometimes an adult did, too.

"Hey cowboy, whatcha doing?" a familiar voice called out. One that sent shivers of excitement down Daniel's entire being.

"Nothing much. How about you?" He grinned and hid his hands behind his back.

Megan arched a brow and tried to see what he was holding behind him. "What's that?" She pointed at his hidden arm.

"Hmm?" Daniel had the look of an angel.

Which only made Megan think he was up to no good. She looked around and watched some of the local kids throwing snowballs. Then she looked back at Daniel and realized the snow on his jeans was from his own participation in the Christmas shenanigans.

She put a finger up and narrowed one eye on him. "If you even think about it, I'll get all of my guys to help me retaliate."

Daniel's grin was so large she could see all of his pearly white teeth, even through the scruff of his unshaven face.

"Who, me?" He put his unhidden hand to his cheek with a mock question on his face. He blinked a few times. "Why, I'd never."

"Uh-huh…" Her comeback was stopped when snow hit her chest.

"Ohhhh, Mr. Caruthers is in big trouble," one of the boys called out.

"Man, don't you know you should never hit your girl with a snowball? Women can be so cruel when they fight back." Another tried to hide his laughter behind his hand.

The rest all snickered and pointed at Daniel.

"You could learn a thing or two from these boys, Mr. Caruthers." Megan put her fists on her hips. "I hope your life insurance premiums are paid up. And just remember, men who end up on Santa's naughty list get no presents." She arched an imperious brow and turned to walk away.

Fear entered Daniel's heart. "Wait, I didn't hurt you, did I?" The last thing he wanted to do was hurt the woman who was starting to mean so much to him. It was his stupid foot-in-mouth disease rearing its ugly head again. He had prayed he'd gotten past it.

When she turned the corner and was out of sight, Daniel turned back to the boys who were still laughing at him. "What do I do?"

"Go after her, you big lump of figgy pudding," Malachi McKinley called out.

"What is figgy pudding?" Jason picked up another handful of snow and began forming a fist-sized ball of snow.

"It's gross, that's what it is." Malachi threw his snowball at Jason before Jason could hit him.

All five of the boys, and Malachi, got back to a serious game of snowball fighting and all thoughts of Daniel and Megan left their heads.

But Daniel was only focused on Megan and ensuring he didn't hurt or offend her. So when he turned the corner, he was shocked when a soft mound of snow hit his face and filled his mouth.

Spluttering, he tried to get the snow out of his mouth and prayed it wasn't yellow, or stained with anything else gross. "What?"

A beautiful laughter that filled his heart with warmth sounded nearby.

"I warned you." Megan stood with one snowball in a hand while the other was fisted at her hip, which jutted out in a way that highlighted her sexy curves.

Daniel put both hands up. "I surrender." Then chuckled when she threw the ball at his chest. It wasn't a hard throw, just enough to let him know she had good aim. "I guess I deserved that."

While laughter filled his heart, Daniel pulled Megan close to him and hugged her. But a hug wasn't the only reason he pulled her close.

"Gross! Get away from me Daniel Caruthers," Megan shrieked when she felt his cold beard rubbing over the side of her head.

"I'm just sharing what you gave me." Daniel continued to rub the snow off his face and onto her hair while she laughed and tried to get away.

Chapter 22

"**D**on't you know it's rude to mess up a woman's hair?" Megan was still laughing and half-heartedly trying to get out of Daniel's arms. Just to keep up the image of being offended. But secretly…well…

Daniel stopped rubbing his face on her hair and put his lips next to her ear. "You know, I think you like it."

And boy howdy, did she. A delicious shiver went up and down her spine and her eyelids fluttered. In a breathy voice she responded, "And I think you enjoy it just as much."

His deep, throaty chuckle sent her heart flittering into overtime. If this were a football game, he would have just scored an extra point. Not quite a touchdown. Maybe he'd get credit for a touchdown if he turned her around and kissed her good and hard.

Whoa, wait. Where did that thought come from? Megan had to clear her throat to get her senses back under control. If she let her hormones lead the way she'd end up in trouble, and probably with a broken heart.

Before either of them could say any more, her phone rang.

"Excuse me, I should get this." Silently she prayed and thanked God for interrupting them.

The moment she looked at the caller ID, all giddiness and lightness fled. Fear and a desire to run filled her, but she wasn't a coward. She hadn't run away when faced with that attack in Afghanistan, and she certainly wouldn't run from this call.

"Hello?" Megan's unsteady voice signaled to Daniel that something was wrong. While she had taken a few steps away from him when she originally went to answer the phone, she now unknowingly walked into his open arms.

His strength and warmth flooded her, and she instantly leaned into his strong chest.

"Ms. Anderson?"

"Yes."

"This is Doctor Rogers. Is Marianne Anderson your mother?"

Fear gripped her, and she prayed that this was *not* the call she had dreaded her entire life. Wasn't this sort of news delivered by the police?

She nodded, then realized he couldn't see her. "Yes, she is. Is my mother alright?"

A heavy sigh came through the phone. "I'm sorry, but I don't know how to tell you this…"

"Oh, please don't tell me she's dead."

The doctor cleared his throat. "No, no. That's not it. At least, not yet. Your mother suffered a grand mal seizure while in jail. She's in a coma, and we aren't sure if she's going to make it."

Megan croaked out a cry, and she put a hand over her mouth.

Daniel took the phone from her hands. "This is Daniel Caruthers. I'm, ah, Megan's friend. What's happened to her mother?"

"What's happened to Ms. Anderson?"

"She's breaking down in tears. Did her mother… I mean." He cleared his throat. "Please tell me how I can help."

"Bring her here as fast as you can. Her mother's in a coma and we don't know if she'll pull through. We should know more by tomorrow, but… I hate to say it, but she might not make it through the night.”

“Thank you, Doctor. We’ll be there as soon as we can.” Daniel hung up the phone and realized he didn’t know where the doctor was calling from. He looked at the caller ID; the doctor had called from her mother’s phone.

“Megan, do you know where your mother is?” Daniel still held her tightly and ran a hand down her back, trying to give her as much of his strength as possible.

She nodded.

“Alright, let’s get out of here and I’ll drive you to her.”

Megan sat mutely in the truck as they drove to the Crooked Arrow Ranch. She knew she needed to pack a bag and let Jerod know what was going on, but how could she find the words? Tears ran down her face, and Daniel handed her a tissue from the box in the center console of his truck.

“Some Christmas this is turning out to be.” The words only came as they pulled into her driveway. If her mother died before Christmas, well, she didn’t want to think about what she’d do. This was turning out to be the worst Christmas she’d ever had. And Megan had experienced more than her fair share of rotten Christmases. Some years she didn’t even celebrate.

This year, she’d thought it would be different. Even with Sam and his onery attitude, she still expected this to be one of the best years ever to celebrate the birth of her Lord and Savior, Jesus Christ. She’d even been enjoying all of the seasonal festivities, like snowball fights, craft fairs, and sleigh rides. Oh, the sleigh rides.

Megan turned to Daniel and noted the serious way he was looking straight ahead. Was she expecting too much from him? “You know, I can get myself to Richland. I know this is a very busy time at the tree farm.”

He shook his head. "No, you aren't going to drive all day and most of the night all alone." He turned and gazed intently into her eyes. "I'm going to be with you."

A tiny smile twitched at the edge of her mouth. This was a real man. The sort of man who could take care of a fiercely independent woman like her.

Why didn't she see it sooner?

Within an hour, her bags were packed, Jerod had told her he had everything under control, and she was off with Daniel to get his bag packed. Neither knew how long they'd be gone, but she couldn't worry about that now.

The men at the Crooked Arrow were in good hands with Jerod. Megan knew that. But what about the tree farm?

"Daniel, how are you going to leave the tree farm? Isn't this your busiest week of the year?"

He took one hand off the steering wheel and reached over to hold hers. "Don't worry about it. Cody has it all under control. While you packed I called him and left him a message. And with Jerod promising to help out, there shouldn't be any issues that all of them together can't handle."

"Are you sure? I don't want you to get in trouble or lose your job because of my family drama." Needing his touch, she held his hand tightly.

"This isn't family drama. This is a true emergency. Cody knows how important family is. And honestly, I think he'd fire me if I didn't support you right now."

Megan bit her lower lip and nodded. "Cody's a good man. Sadie's one lucky woman."

Daniel squeezed her hand and they drove to his house in silence. It wasn't but another thirty minutes until he was on the I-90 heading to Richland. It seemed men could throw clothes and toiletries into a bag in only two shakes.

Women, on the other hand, had so many things to pack. And they needed to make sure they folded their clothes and not throw them all willy nilly into a bag only to be wrinkled when they arrived at their destination. Even though Megan knew this wasn't the time to worry about her appearance, she also knew her mother would expect Megan to be well dressed with makeup and hair done. Just like she always did.

And Megan was going to do whatever it took to please her mother right now. If wearing nice clothes and putting on makeup, something she didn't do much of on the ranch, would help her mother, she'd do it. Plus, the last thing she wanted to hear come out of her mother's mouth as soon as she woke up was a complaint about the way she looked.

With all of the stress from the day and the past week, it didn't take Megan long to nod off while Daniel drove. When they were nearing Cor d'Alene, Idaho, she felt someone pulling her from her perfect dream. She didn't want to leave it. In the peace of sleep she'd dreamt she was a child again, and her mom had married her dad. The three of them were celebrating Christmas Day.

Tons of presents still filled the space beneath the Christmas tree, but Megan had already opened up so many that wrapping paper covered the room and she was tired. In her dream, she lay against her dad's shoulders. His face was blurred enough that she couldn't make out his features, but she knew he had strong shoulders and loving arms that held her tight. She felt safe and drifted off to sleep in her daddy's arms, thinking that she was so lucky to have the perfect family.

But when she awoke and reality slammed into her like a speeding locomotive, she felt wetness dripping down her cheeks.

"Hey, it's alright. We're gonna make it in time. And your mother's going to pull through." With the center console in the way, Daniel couldn't pull her close enough to him, but he could take her hand in his. They stayed quiet until he pulled off the highway and into the parking lot of a large gas station.

Once the truck was in park, he got out and moved around to open her door. Megan wrapped her arms around his neck and he stood there holding her while she got herself together.

"I'm sorry. I'm a wreck today. Please don't mind me." Megan wiped the tears from her face and sniffed. Then she turned around and took more tissue.

Daniel moved her over and climbed into the seat with her in his lap. "Don't worry, I'm here for you. It's not surprising that you're so emotional—this is a really a tough time. And not knowing what's going to happen is the worst."

"I wish"—she sighed—"I wish I could tell Santa my Christmas wish and he'd make it all come true." If she could, she'd wish her dream was reality, and that this reality was a nightmare. Although, she'd like to keep Daniel in her life. He was the only good thing she had right now.

"What do you say we pray and then go get some food? I don't know about you, but I could use some sustenance right about now. And a Dr. Pepper." Daniel lowered his head and began to pray.

"Thank you." Megan folded her hands in her lap and lowered her head as well.

"Dear Heavenly Father, right now everything is so confusing and not knowing what's going to happen to Marianne makes it so much worse. I ask that you please put a hedge of protection around her. Heal her body and mind. And please give the doctors the knowledge they need to pull her out of the coma. Also, help Megan. Give her peace to get through the coming days, no matter the outcome. Help her to rely on you to give her strength. And help me to be the shoulder she can cry on. All these things I ask in your Son's holy and precious name, amen."

"Amen. Thank you, Daniel. I'm really glad you came with me. I don't know if I could have made this drive alone."

Daniel kissed her hand. "Yes, you could have. You're stronger than you think. And with God on your side, you can do anything. Just remember you get your strength from your savior."

They got out of the truck and he took Megan's hand. They walked together into the store with Megan feeling as though a ton of bricks had been taken off her shoulders. She leaned into him and kissed his cheek. "Thank you, you really are the best friend a woman could ever have."

A moment of pain flashed across his features, and she wondered what she'd done.

"I'm glad I could be here for you." Daniel rubbed his thumb across the back of her hand.

Chapter 23

Friend? Really, *friend*? He'd been thrown into the friend zone. How was he ever going to get out of that? Obviously they couldn't go out on a date while they were seeing to Megan's mom, but calling him her best friend? Ouch. Way to stab a guy through the heart.

Daniel mulled over her words as Megan fell back asleep right after they got back on the road. They weren't too far from the hospital, and Daniel didn't have the heart to keep her awake. She needed her sleep after all the highs and lows of the day. Mostly the lows. He wasn't a big crier, but he knew enough about women to know that when they cried as much as she had that day, the woman was going to need a ton of sleep.

Even though it hurt as much as if she'd stabbed him right through the heart, he was going to do his best to be her friend. Or buddy, or whatever it was she needed. Maybe when this was all over, Megan would want more.

When he saw the sign for the hospital exit, he nudged Megan to wake her up. "Megan, we're almost there."

"Huh?" The bleary-eyed young woman rubbed at her eyes and stretched in her seat. Then she looked around. "Where are we?"

"We've made it to Richland. The next exit is the hospital." Daniel kept his eyes on the road. It wasn't much past rush hour and there were more cars on the road than he was used to.

"I'm sorry. I meant to help with the driving." She looked around at their surroundings. "I can't believe I slept the whole way."

"No worries. You needed to rest in order to get your strength up. Who knows how long they'll let you stay in your mom's room, but I know you don't want to sleep and miss her waking up." As they drove, he kept praying for a miracle and for Marianne to wake up when her daughter entered the room.

When they parked and entered the hospital, a nice elderly nurse guided them to Marianne's room. She stopped outside the glass-enclosed room. "Only one person at a time can visit." She looked between the two.

Daniel took a step back and held his arms up. "I'll wait out here, if that's alright?"

The nurse gave him a sweet smile and pointed to a room only a few feet away. It was the family room for those waiting to take turns visiting patients in the intensive care unit.

Daniel kissed the top of Megan's head. "I'll wait for you over there. Take your time."

The elderly nurse walked away, and Daniel headed for a comfy chair.

When he entered the sterile room, he was disappointed. The hard seats were obviously meant to ensure that people didn't stay long. Instead of sitting, he paced the short room.

Every time he walked by the door, he looked out into the ICU and noticed doctors and nurses bustling about. There were ten rooms made up of glassed-in walls and doors. There were drapes for privacy, but only one room had them closed. The rest were opened up so that the nurses' station in the middle of the room had a good view of the patients.

His attention was caught by a moving green dot on a monitor hanging from the ceiling above the nurses' station. It looked like each room had its own monitor, and vitals were constantly being updated on the screens.

Not all of the rooms were in use. So only six monitors were currently displaying the information the nurses needed to keep track of.

Daniel decided to head to the nurse and see if he could get any information about Marianne's health. "Excuse me, miss?" He looked at the badge of a younger woman standing behind the counter. "Miss Marple. Can you tell me how Marianne Anderson is doing?"

Miss Marple turned her head and eyed him up and down. His clothes were rumpled from the five-hour drive, but other than that he didn't think he looked too bad.

"Are you a relative?"

He shook his head. "No, I'm here with her daughter." He pointed to Megan. "She's Megan Anderson."

"I'm sorry sir, but unless Megan gives us the okay, I can't say anything about the patient's health. HIPAA regulations are very clear. You understand, right?"

Daniel sighed. "Yeah, I do. Thanks." He looked up at screen number three, which was Marianne's room number, and noted that her vitals seemed strong. At least she looked like she might make it through. But what did he know? He was only a Christmas tree farm foreman. He wasn't a doctor.

But his uncle was a type of doctor. Uncle Steve may have only treated animals, but that didn't mean Daniel hadn't learned a thing or two. Growing up with a veterinarian did that. And Marianne's pulse seemed strong. As did her constant heart rate. Although, he had no idea what all the squiggly lines meant for her brain.

Anxiety began to creep in and Daniel went to sit on the hard plastic chair to pray. He prayed that God would heal Marianne, not just from the seizure, but also from her drug addiction. He couldn't imagine what life must have been like for a woman to become so addicted to drugs that ever after several attempts at rehab, she still went back to them.

Why didn't a mother choose to be healthy for her daughter? His mom had been single and she'd worked hard to provide him with a loving, stable home. It wasn't always easy, which was why they'd moved in with his uncle, but still, his mother was always there for him. She could have chosen to numb her own pain, but she didn't. Maybe putting the welfare of her son ahead of her own was what got her through the difficult times.

Megan had said something once about the wounded vets and needing to help others in order to help themselves. Could it be that when anyone, veteran or civilian, was hurting, putting others first would help enough for them to heal of their own wounds?

Thinking back through the years, and seeing how his mom was always there for him and dumped a few men who weren't good to him just to protect him, it made his heart ache to see his own mom again. When Christmas was over, he was going to take a trip out to see her and thank her for choosing him over anything else that could have numbed her sadness.

But now he needed to put someone else's needs above his own. And that meant getting over the disappointment of being put in the friend zone. Daniel was going to be the best friend he could to Megan—and Marianne, if she made it through this.

As he prayed some more for the wisdom to know how to help the Anderson women, he heard a throat clear. When he looked up, the nurse from earlier, who wouldn't tell him anything, smiled.

Daniel stood up and ran a hand through his messy hair. "Any news?"

"Yes, great news. Marianne woke up. The doctor is with her now, but I think her daughter—what did you say her name was?" The nurse had a thoughtful look on her face.

"Megan."

"Yes, Megan. She could use your help right now. She's, ah"—the nurse looked over her shoulder—"she needs a strong shoulder."

Daniel followed Nurse Marple's gaze and saw that Megan was crumpled in a heap on a chair with her shoulders shaking and her face in her hands. "Thanks." He took three long strides and was out the door, practically running to Megan.

Once he was next to her, indecision warred within him. Should he just pull her up and hold her tight? Or should he sit down and put an arm around her, like a friend would do? All thoughts escaped him when she turned red, teary eyes on him.

"Daniel." She sobbed.

He didn't even think. Instead, his instincts kicked in and he took her by her shoulders and pulled her into his warm embrace. "Megan. I'm here."

He wasn't sure why she was such a mess. Her mother had woken up. That was a good thing, wasn't it? Instead of asking, he just let her cry it out. Maybe it was just all of the stress and fear coming out? Again he reckoned he knew next to nothing about women, so how could he know?

After a few minutes, her breathing started to slow and she sniffed a couple of times. Megan pulled out some tissues from her bag and cleaned herself up. Daniel waited until she was ready to speak. "Thank you. I don't know how I would have gotten through this without you." Megan sniffed again and looked at Daniel.

Her eyes and face were red and swollen, but that didn't matter to him. Daniel still thought she was the most beautiful woman he'd ever seen. A part of him ached for her, but the other part rejoiced that her mom had woken up.

"She didn't recognize me," she admitted in a small voice.

"Who? Your mom?"

Megan's head was back on Daniel's shoulder, and he felt her nod. "Yes."

"What did the doctor say?"

"I don't know anything yet. When she woke up I pushed the button and started talking to her, but she looked so confused. Fear crossed her features, and she looked around before asking who I was." Megan hiccupped.

Daniel ran a hand down the back of Megan's head, lightly stroking her hair. "Maybe it was because she wasn't quite out of the coma yet?"

"Maybe. I hope that's all it was. But the doctor came in quickly and one of the nurses ushered me out before I could ask any questions." Megan pulled out of his embrace again and looked up into his face. "Do you think she'll remember me?"

"I do." Daniel nodded. "I think she's just going to need a little bit to get her wits about her and she'll be right as rain."

They both watched the room as doctors, nurses, and who knew who else came and went. No one even noticed the two of them sitting off to the side watching and waiting.

After what felt like hours, but was probably less than one hour, Nurse Marple walked over with a small smile. "Miss Anderson, the doctor is ready to speak with you." She turned to look at Daniel, then back to Megan. "You can have your friend with you if you like."

"Yes, I need Daniel." Megan stood and took Daniel's hand.

He stood up and squeezed her hand, but stayed quiet.

They followed the nurse to a small room behind the nurses' station. Daniel had noticed it earlier, but the door was closed so he thought it must be a supply closet, or something along those lines.

Turns out it wasn't.

"Miss Anderson, I'm Doctor Leavitt." He motioned for them to sit in the two chairs in front of his desk.

Chapter 24

This was it. This was when Megan was going to find out if her mother would ever know her or not. She gulped as she sat down next to Daniel, holding tight to his hand.

She licked her dry lips and wished she'd had a moment to get water.

"Miss Anderson, I understand that when your mother first awoke, she didn't recognize you." Doctor Leavitt waited for Megan to respond.

She nodded.

The doctor cleared his throat. "That's not uncommon. But I want to assure you that we are going to do everything we can to help your mother through her recovery. There's still a lot of testing to do, and sadly…waiting."

Megan slouched. "So she still doesn't recognize me?"

"Not exactly. She knows she had a daughter, but she can't remember much yet." He held his hand up to keep Megan from speaking. "Keep in mind that her brain has undergone a lot of trauma. Her neurons are rewriting themselves to bypass the injured areas. This takes time."

"Will you have to do surgery?" The fear that her mom would need to undergo brain surgery caused Megan to held even tighter to Daniel's strong hand.

The doctor shook his head. "Not at this time. We are going to do an MRI of her brain as well as a CAT scan just to make sure she's not bleeding. But I think you should feel positive. That fact that she woke up so quickly is a very good sign."

Megan bit the inside of her lip and took a few deep breaths. "You think she'll get back all of her cognitive abilities?"

"I can't say any more until we've done a few tests. This is going to take a few hours, and I'm afraid you won't be able to see her." The doctor looked between the two. "Have you checked into a hotel yet?"

This time Daniel took the reins. "Not yet, but I do have a reservation for us nearby."

"Good, good." The doctor nodded his approval. "Why don't you go and get settled in your rooms and take a nap? I'll have a nurse call you when your mother is ready for visitors again."

Megan stood up. "I can't stay here?"

"No, your mom won't be in her room again for several hours. Then she's going to need rest. And you will need rest if you plan to be strong for your mother. Please, go to the hotel and sleep for a while. Eat lunch." The doctor stood and put his hand out to Megan. "I promise we'll call you just as soon your mother is ready for a visit. It will have to be brief, though."

Megan nodded. "Of course. And thank you, Doctor."

Daniel shook the doctor's hand and gave him a nod before taking Megan out to the truck.

The next three days flew by in a blur of activity. Megan's mom was getting better, and on the third day, all had reason to rejoice.

On the fourth day, they both walked into Marianne's hospital room, still in the ICU. "Hi, Mom. How…" Megan stopped dead in her tracks with her mouth hanging down.

Sitting up in bed with a smile and a look of recognition, Marianne reached her arms out toward her daughter.

"Sweetheart! It's so good to see you."

"Mom? You remember me?" Megan took halting steps as her heart raced. While she wanted to believe her mom's memories were back, she also didn't want to get her hopes up.

Daniel stood behind Megan, lending her his support. She felt his strong presence and knew she could do this. She *had* to do this.

"Yes, sweetie. It's all coming back in bits and pieces, but the one thing I remember most is you. I'm so sorry I couldn't remember until now." She put her arms down, looking like she might cry as her eyes glistened with unshed tears.

"Oh, Mom." Megan ran to her mother's bed and hugged her.

"Be careful, she's still recovering." Daniel stood next to Megan and put a hand on her back.

Marianne Anderson looked older and smaller laying in the bed covered in blankets and wearing a hospital gown that had to be two sizes too large for her frame. The woman looked almost emaciated with her wrist bones and shoulder bones sticking out. And her hair was a stringy, dishwater brown that hung limp around her shoulders.

Her mother used to pride herself on having luscious light-brown hair with just the right amount of natural wave. When Megan was a young girl, her mom would sit in front of her mirror every morning and every night and brush it out for at least ten minutes. Then she'd brush Megan's hair, teaching her how to take care of her beauty. Her mom had put so much stock into a woman's beauty. How would she handle how she looked today?

Megan admonished herself for not going to her mom last week when she got the first call about her being in the hospital for a heart attack. "Oh, Mom. Do you think you may have had an actual heart attack last week? Or was it just a coincidence?"

"I think it was just as the original attending doctor said—angina," a deep voice said behind her. "But it should have been a wake-up call to your mother that her body wasn't in good shape."

Megan turned around to see the doctor. He was a tall man with a full head of brown hair and gray streaks running throughout. Megan and Daniel had wondered about him and decided he must only be in his mid-forties. The stress of his job must have caused him to gray prematurely.

But his eyes were a warm, chocolate brown with little laugh lines. He always had a smile when he saw Megan and Daniel, which helped them both to feel more comfortable in his presence.

Marianne shrank even more in her bedding and Megan worried her mom might disappear if she sank any lower into her covers. "I know. I really messed up this time. I'm very lucky I didn't die."

"No, you were blessed." Megan pursed her lips and prayed God would give her the right words. "There is no such thing as luck. We all have a time and date set for us. Even though you seem to want to tempt God's hand, He has kept you alive. For now. But remember, Mom, that God gave us free will. If you're so hell-bent on dying, eventually He will allow it."

Tears ran down Marianne's face, and Megan felt awful.

Daniel must have known how she felt, for he put a supportive arm around her.

"She's not wrong." The doctor's agreement with her shocked Megan.

Both Daniel and Megan looked to the man who now stood at the foot of Marianne's bed, looking at a computer display to the side. The other side of the bed had a plethora of medical devices that Megan had no clue about. The only thing she really understood was the IV in her mom's arm. Two bags hung from it now. When they'd first arrived there were five different bags hanging there, all draining into her mother's veins.

"Please don't tell me you're one of those Bible-thumpers, too?" Marianne rolled her eyes and glared at her doctor.

Megan knew her mother wasn't a believer. The only reason Megan believed was because of her grandmother's influence when she was a little girl. Back then, a few of her friends would take her to church and out to lunch with their family Sunday afternoons. She was so thankful that God had found a way to reach her early on in life. She only wished her mother also knew the saving grace of Jesus.

Just then, a nurse wearing a Santa hat came into the room and greeted everyone. "Good morning, today we're going to have a little Christmas celebration out at the nurses' station. All family and patients who are able are welcome to join us."

Megan looked to Daniel, who grinned in return.

"I think that would be fun." Daniel turned to the doctor. "Is Marianne able to get into a wheelchair and attend?"

The past two days the nursing staff had helped Marianne get into a chair, but she hadn't done any real walking yet. The doctor just wanted Marianne to sit up in a chair and get out of bed for a few hours a day to help her blood flow.

Dr. Leavitt considered the question for a moment, then nodded. "I think a few minutes in a wheelchair might be good for her."

"So, does this mean she's really getting better?" Megan put her hands together in front of her chest in a pleading motion. She wanted nothing more than to see her mom on the road to recovery.

He held up his hand. "I said a few minutes. I don't want Marianne to overdo it. Instead of sweet punch, I'd rather you stick to apple juice for now. Your stomach may not do well with a lot of sugar."

They discussed what she could and should eat, as well as what she should avoid. When the nurse came back to help Marianne into her morning chair, she also brought a protein shake. "The doctor wanted you to try this. You need protein, but your stomach still isn't doing well with much more than soup and bread. Take it in small sips and see how your stomach reacts."

When the time for the Christmas party rolled around, everyone was excited. Marianne looked even better than she had all day.

"Mom, are you looking forward to the party?" Megan asked.

A large smile spread across Marianne's face and even touched her eyes. "Yes, I am. I'd forgotten how close it was to Christmas."

"I think the nurses have been decorating the ward all day long. It kinda looks like Rudolph came for a visit and brought a lot of friends." Daniel winked at Marianne.

This time, Megan didn't mind him winking. In fact, warmth spread through her as she realized Daniel had been a wonderful help to her and her mom. His winking wasn't so much flirting as it was friendly.

Marianne ran a hand down her recently washed hair and returned his smile as her cheeks turned pink. She was starting to look like her old self again. She must really be on the road to recovery.

Megan insisted on pushing the wheelchair when it was time to join the party.

Real Christmas joy enveloped Megan as she entered the breakroom and saw all of the decorations. She thought the Christmas décor at the nurses' station was going a bit overboard, but this room? Daniel was right—Rudolph had come to town.

The nurses' station had glittery Christmas garland wrapped all around the large desk in the middle of the room. There were six computer monitors on the workstations and each of them had been wrapped with Christmas paper, leaving open the part of the screen needed to do their work. But on the back of the monitor was a different-colored ribbon and bow, the fancy kind that took a device to make.

There were also decorations hanging from the ceiling. The popular red Christmas truck with trees in the bed, along with a few Christmas gnomes, decorated the desk and tabletops wherever there was an open space. There were even candy canes on the garland and a candy dish on opposite sides of the desk.

So when they entered the breakroom, where there were homemade food and drinks, Megan was utterly surprised to see that even more decorations had been hung all over. Where they had found the time to do this and take care of their patients, she'd never know. Nurses were the lifeblood of the hospital, and she was truly thankful that they had gone the extra mile to throw this party for their patients and their families.

"We will do this every week until the new year. We have so many patients and families coming through. A lot of them need the extra cheer." One of the nurses that Megan had seen but not spoken to was telling another patient about their month of Christmas cheer.

"Look, can you name them all?" Daniel pointed to the wall where large, almost life-size cutouts of the nine reindeer, headed by Rudolph, adorned the walls.

"Pft, child's play." Megan rolled her eyes and looked to the wall. "They've got them out of order."

Marianne sighed. "That's my girl."

Daniel crossed his arms over his chest and realized he was about to see a master at work. "Okay, if they're out of order, then point to each and name them. Then tell me the order they should be in."

The room went silent, and all eyes focused on the trio.

Megan started to feel a bit awkward with everyone staring at her.

Miss Marple grinned. "I was hoping someone would notice. Care to put them in their proper order?"

"Who, me?" Megan stared at the nurse with wide eyes and tapped her chest.

"Who else? You seem to be the only one who knows how it should go." The nurse took a few steps closer, then whispered, "Give them a little show. Something to liven the mood around here."

Daniel put his arms down by his sides and chuckled. "Looks like Megan's the cowgirl of the hour."

"Of course, isn't she always? Just like her momma." Marianne beamed with pride at her daughter.

Nervous laughter bubbled up and Megan took a few steps to the wall. As she eyed each of the reindeer, she mentally picked out the team in order. Once they were all sitting on a tabletop, Nurse Marple brought her some sticky gum for repositioning them on the wall.

"Well, of course Rudolph is out front." She pursed her lips and looked over her shoulder at a couple of the nurses who were giggling.

One of them spoke up. "Yeah, that was intentional. We wanted to see if anyone noticed at least Rudolph was in the wrong spot."

A middle-aged man looked back and forth between Megan and the nurse. "How can you tell it's Rudolph?"

Megan was about to say something flippant, but bit her lower lip instead.

One of the other women guests spoke up first. "You can always tell Rudolph by the red nose. No other reindeer has one."

The man nodded. "Of course, I'll have to remember that when my baby's born."

A woman who must have been his wife walked up to him, put an arm around his waist, and beamed up at him. He put his hands on her stomach. They were there with an elderly gentleman who was in a wheelchair. But he looked as though he was in much better shape than Marianne. He didn't even have an IV pole and bag with him, unlike Marianne. Her IV bags were attached to a pole on the back of her wheelchair.

Only four of the nine patients in the ward seemed to be at the party. Megan realized the others were most likely too ill to get into a wheelchair.

As Megan went back to work positioning the reindeer cut-outs on the wall, Daniel went to the food and drink table and put a tiny plate together. When he walked back to Marianne, her eyes glowed.

"Is that for me?"

"Nah, I didn't think you'd want anything. You know, since all you've wanted so far is soup." He winked at her and handed her the plate. "Here's a little selection of bread and a sugar-free cookie. I hope it tastes good."

The first thing Marianne tried was the cookie. "Mmmm, this is really good. I wouldn't mind getting the recipe for these. What is it?"

"It's a high-protein peanut butter cookie." Daniel watched as she finished it off. Then he looked between the table, Megan, and Marianne. "I'll grab you another one."

Not only did he get her one, but he also picked one up for himself as Megan finished the display on the wall.

"So, do you know their names?" Megan asked when she went back to her mom and Daniel.

Daniel looked at the reindeer positioned just right for pulling Santa's sleigh, and pointed. "Rudolph, Dasher, Dancer, Prancer, Vixen, Comet, Cupid, Donner, and Blitzen."

Megan grinned. "Good eyes."

"I do know how to read." Daniel puffed out his chest.

Marianne's forehead crinkled and she pursed her lips. "Read?"

Megan pointed the reindeer. "Look at their collars."

Her mother squinted and leaned forward a bit. Then her face relaxed and she sat back. "Hah! That's cheating."

Nurse Marple came over grinning. "It's not cheating if the collars are marked with their names. It's paying attention. Good job, Megan."

"Thanks."

"I'd have noticed if I wasn't confined to this silly wheelchair." Marianne huffed and tried to cross her arms over her chest, but had to put them back down when her IV got in the way.

"I think it's time Miss Marianne went back to her room for a nap." Nurse Marple turned worried eyes on her patient. "You two stay and enjoy the party. I'll take your mother back and get her settled."

"Well, I'd say my mom is getting back to her old self." Megan sighed and watched as the nurse wheeled her out of the party room.

Chapter 25

D aniel had been in touch with Cody throughout the week. He felt bad for leaving them shorthanded, but when Cody told him to not worry and to focus on Megan and her mother for the umpteenth time, he relaxed. Then he realized he'd gone all week without his favorite treat for this time of year.

"Megan?" They were eating breakfast at their hotel before heading over to see Megan's mom. She was being moved to a regular room today and they had asked that Megan and Daniel take their time coming to the hospital, so both decided a lazy breakfast was due.

"Hm?" she asked in between bites of her Belgian waffle.

"What do you think about heading over to a local coffee shop when we're done and getting a couple PSLs?" He had wanted to eat out at a nicer breakfast place, but free breakfast with the room was hard to pass up. Especially since everything was so expensive already.

Megan swallowed the food in her mouth, dabbed at her lips, and tilted her head. "You do know that nothing you get outside of the Frenchtown Roasting Company will be as good as Lottie's drinks, right?"

He sighed. "I know, but I feel like I'm losing out if I don't have a couple of PSLs this week, and since I haven't had any yet…" Daniel shrugged.

Megan grinned. "Alright, I guess I could go for a PSL. Even though it isn't my favorite drink."

With furrowed brows, Daniel looked at her questioningly. "What is your favorite drink?"

"Peppermint mocha, of course." She rolled her eyes. "Everyone knows it's the best drink on the planet. Some places even serve it year-round."

"Not Lottie."

"Oh, don't I know it. A few of us ladies back home have tried and tried to get her to serve it outside of Christmas, but she won't." Megan scowled.

Daniel chuckled. "I know, she's a stickler for holiday drinks being served during the holiday season only. But"—he put a finger in the air—"down the street is one of those fancy coffee shops. I bet we can both get some great drinks. What do you say?"

Megan agreed, and once they finished their breakfast they drove down the street.

Daniel watched as Megan's eyes bulged when she walked inside the coffee shop. There had to be at least ten people in line waiting to order.

"I don't know about this. We need to get to the hospital." Megan looked around and stopped at the end of the line.

"We still have time, let's get a drink and hang out here. We need to talk about your plans." He had spoken with the doctor yesterday, and the police. What he'd learned had him a bit worried for Megan. If they could get a spot in the corner, they could talk with some semblance of privacy. Especially since the place was so loud, he doubted anyone would be able to hear them.

As they stood in line and waited, Megan noticed an empty corner table. "Look." She pointed. "I'll go grab that table. You know what to get me, right?"

He nodded.

Knowing the wait would take a while after he ordered, Daniel went and joined Megan. Now was as good a time as any to get this started. Although, a pit opened up in his stomach as he tried to form the words that needed to come out.

"I know that look." Megan pursed her lips. "You have bad news."

"Yes, sorta." Daniel winced and rubbed the back of his neck.

"I know we need to head home, but I want to make sure my mom's settled in her new room and the latest round of tests come back with good news." She folded her hands in front of her on the table.

"Um, that's not what I wanted to talk about, but you're right. We do need to head home soon. Tomorrow would be a good day to go." Daniel looked to the baristas to see if their coffees were ready yet; they weren't.

A frown appeared on Megan's face. "I think that's too soon. Maybe in a few more days? I need to find out more about her *other* situation as well."

"Yeah, about that. I meant to say something last night, but..." He shrugged. "I think I chickened out."

Megan sat up tall and glared at Daniel. "You better tell me what you know, and now, buster."

"Big Sky Christmas!" the barista bellowed out. Daniel had given the tree farm's name instead of their names, since it would stand out better.

"Be right back." Daniel ran away like a dog with his tail between his legs. He still wasn't ready to discuss this, but he had to. The doctor wanted to speak with Megan this morning, and he had to prepare her.

Once he was seated with their drinks, he took a deep breath and looked at Megan. "The doctor wants to send your mom to a medical rehab facility next week."

Megan blinked. "Yeah, I kinda expected that. Hospitals don't keep patients in their beds for long—they tend to send them out to rehab facilities that don't cost as much for treatment."

"And, it's more of a high-security type of place." He waited for her to soak this in.

"Why?"

"The police are working with the DA on a deal for your mom. I don't know much about the details, but until it's all handled the doctor didn't want to release her to sit in jail. Not when she's still so weak. So he arranged for a special facility for your mom. They'll have more security than normal and she won't be allowed to leave until the courts say she can." This was the part Daniel didn't agree with. But he also didn't understand everything going on at the courthouse.

"Why didn't he tell me himself?" Megan took a long drink and then scowled at Daniel.

"He did go looking for you, but he couldn't find you. He told me this before he left for the day. Dr. Leavitt wants to speak with you today about it all." Maybe Daniel should have said something right away, but he wanted Megan and her mother to enjoy the evening. If he'd had said anything to either of them, Daniel knew it would have ruined the good time Megan was having getting to know her mother again.

Marianne had refused to call her boyfriend, and when he tried calling her, she denied his call. Megan had told him that this was a first. It seemed like Marianne really had turned a corner. But she did still need to deal with the criminal charges against her.

"You should have told me right away, last night when you saw me." Megan crossed her arms over her chest. The hot glare she gave him would have been enough to melt him if he were a snowman.

Daniel wiggled in his seat, realizing for the first time that he had made a big mistake. They had come so far in their friendship, and he prayed this wouldn't set them back. "Please forgive me, Megan. I didn't mean to keep anything from you." He sighed. "I just didn't want to ruin the good mood you and your mother were in last night. The two of you were bonding and it seemed that this could wait."

"You had no right to keep this from me, or my mom. Does she know anything about this yet?"

"I don't know. The doctor asked that we see him after your mom was moved to her new room to discuss it all." Shrinking in his seat, Daniel took another sip of his PSL. At least it was a good drink, and still hot.

Megan stood up abruptly and glared at him. "Come on. We have to go, now." Without waiting for him to at least stand, she turned on her heels and walked out the door, leaving her drink behind.

With a heavy sigh and a quick prayer asking for strength and guidance, Daniel stood up and took her drink with him when he left.

<h1 style="text-align:center">Chapter 26</h1>

"How could he?" Megan exclaimed under her breath as she stood next to the truck waiting for Daniel. She fumed over this latest. When he was saying stupid things it wasn't really hurting anyone, but this was too far. And it was hurting her mother's chances at getting good help.

Megan wondered how anyone could get decent help recovering if they were in a prison detention facility. She pictured her mom being handcuffed to her bed and nurses ignoring her calls for help.

By the time Daniel made it to the truck, she was struggling to keep her tears at bay. This was all too much. She should have come on her own. Maybe she should send him back to Montana while she stayed here doing whatever she could to help her mom. Plane tickets back to Montana from Eastern Washington weren't too bad. And the view from her hotel—of the river flowing lazily past her window—was actually quite peaceful.

Maybe she could even take a leave of absence and get a temporary job here while she helped her mom get through everything.

Daniel opened her truck door for her and handed her the peppermint mocha she'd left behind. Without a word, she got inside and he closed her door. As they headed to the hospital she continued to make plans to stay in town while she ignored Daniel.

That, that…cowboy! she thought to herself. He was so infuriating. How could he try to control what she did and did not know about her mom?

When he had pulled into a parking space, Daniel put the truck in park. "Megan, I really didn't mean to keep anything from you. I just hadn't seen either of you smile like that all week and I didn't want to cast a cloud over your joy last night. I'm truly sorry. I won't keep anything from you again."

Her anger began to deflate, though she did try to hold onto it for a few more minutes before she realized he may have a point.

It was a good night for both her and her mom. Megan had started to see her old mom coming out, and her normally ditzy persona was all but gone. The drugs were making their way out of her system and her thinking was clearing up. Not to mention the healing from the seizure. It was the best night she'd had with her mom in years, if not a decade or more.

Her nostrils flared and she relaxed. "You're forgiven. But please don't decide what I should and shouldn't know about my own family ever again." Megan turned to look at him. "I mean it. This is my life, not yours."

She noticed the pain ripple across his features before he shuttered his emotions. Daniel nodded. "Of course."

"Alright, let's get inside and see what's really going on." Not wanting to wait for him to open her door, Megan stepped out of the truck and met Daniel at the hood.

While they walked inside, she wondered what he had to be hurt about. Did she hurt his feelings when she expressed how she felt? He was the one who had done wrong, not her. And her response had been completely normal.

If that was true, then why did she feel guilty? As she pondered *how* she'd reacted to him, Doctor Leavitt walked up and greeted them both.

"I just left your mother and she's resting comfortably in her new room. Would you care to come to my office so we can discuss her situation?" The doctor led them to his office on the third floor.

"Is there a cop or something outside her room? What's really going on? Daniel told me just this morning"—she pursed her lips and gave him a side glance—"what you said about my mom going to a sort of prison hospital."

Doctor Leavitt held up his hands. "It's not a prison. She's not been convicted of anything yet, but the local district attorney wants to keep an eye on her while she recovers."

Megan furrowed her brows. "Then what sort of institution are you sending her to?"

"It's a rehab facility designed for low-level prisoners and those awaiting trial. While there is a high level of security, your mom will receive top-notch care. She won't be treated like a criminal or anything of that sort." The earnest expression on the doctor's face helped to calm Megan's fears.

"Will I be able to visit her?"

Doctor Leavitt nodded.

Megan noticed out of the corner of her eye that Daniel was fidgeting. He looked as though he wanted to ask something but was holding his tongue. "Daniel, did you have something to say?"

With a short cough, Daniel proceeded. "What is the DA saying about Marianne's situation, exactly?"

"I'm not really sure. All I know is that they have a court document requiring her to be sent to the facility I told you about. I think the district attorney wants to speak with Marianne and her attorney about the situation."

"Alright, thanks. I'll call my mom's attorney today, after I see her. Thank you, Doctor." Megan stood and shook the doctor's hand.

Daniel followed suit.

After several conversations with her mom and her mom's attorney, Megan decided she needed to head back to Montana and get her own truck and come back. It looked like this was going to take a while.

She also needed to have a serious discussion with Daniel.

The next day as Daniel drove them back to Montana, he risked her ire by asking her what she planned to do.

"I'm going to ask for a leave of absence. If Jerod can't do that, then I'll quit. My mom needs me right now. And it looks as though she might really be ready to make the changes she needs to."

Megan knew that over the past week, she and Daniel had gotten very close. It wasn't that she was still made at him, but her mother needed her more than a man did.

"Daniel, I know we decided to be friends, and I do want that. But…" Megan wasn't sure how to start this conversation. While they had been friends, there was also something more developing. Something that she had no time to deal with.

He cleared his throat. "I'm willing to wait until you come home before we move forward." A trickle of sweat beaded down the side of his face, but he kept his eyes on the road ahead of them.

Megan licked her lips and swallowed hard. "I don't think you should do that."

"What do you mean?" For just a second he took his eyes off the road to look at her.

"Eyes on the road, please." The last thing she needed was a car accident at this point.

He looked forward and Megan noticed his white knuckles on the steering wheel. She sighed. "I don't have time for anything more than looking after my mom right now. Even work is going to take a backseat until things are settled. I…" not knowing what to say, she looked out the side window and blinked back tears. This wasn't what she wanted, but it was what she needed.

"I see." He kept his eyes forward and they drove with very little conversation until Daniel dropped her off at the Crooked Arrow Ranch. "You know, I'm always here. Even if you just need someone to listen."

The last of the anger dissolved and she sighed. "Daniel, you really have a great heart. Thank you so much. I'm sorry the past few days have been so stressful. I'll let you know what happens with Jerod, and my mom."

"Please be sure to keep me up to date on your mom's situation. And I'll pray for her."

Daniel waved as he drove off, thinking this was the last he'd ever see of the beautiful counselor.

Jerod was inside sitting at the kitchen table when Megan had finished taking her bags to her room. "Sit down and tell me what happened." He handed her a fresh cup of coffee fixed just the way she liked, including the peppermint mocha creamer.

"You remembered. Thank you." Megan smiled and took a long sip of the hot coffee. "Mmm, this is exactly what I needed. Thanks."

Jerod sat there with an arched brow as though he knew she was stalling.

"Fine. My mom is getting better. She'll most likely make a full recovery. There are still some minor issues, but the doctor said in time she might get past it."

"I thought with a grand mal seizure people didn't make full recoveries?" The head of the Crooked Arrow Ranch watched her, waiting for her response.

"Well, my mom does have some issues, memory being one of them. She's also still walking slow, so maybe a full recovery is a bit too much to expect." The energy left her and she huddled over her mug of coffee. A small smile tilted up the right side of her face; Jerod had fixed her coffee in the Big Sky Christmas mug. It was her favorite of all the mugs they had in the cupboard.

"What else?" At first Jerod had seemed patient, but now she could tell he wanted the whole story.

"Did you talk to Daniel?"

He shook his head. "Does he have information for me?"

"No, it's just you seem to be waiting for me to say something in particular." Megan bit the inside of her cheek.

Jerod sighed. "I guess I'm expecting you to want more time off. Is that what you're going to ask?"

How in the world could he know that? But, it was Jerod. He was one of the most observant people she'd ever met. If anyone would guess at the truth, it would be him.

She nodded. "I was going to ask for an extended leave of absence to help my mom, but something else is coming to mind."

"Oh really? What's that?"

Megan quirked her lips as she continued with the radical train of thought. "My mom has to do this prison-like rehab. But if she doesn't have to go to jail, I was wondering if she could come live here until she gets back on her feet?" Megan rushed to say more before Jerod could say no. "I'd take care of her. She could even stay in one of the cabins instead of in here."

A long moment of silence passed between them. "I don't know. Your mom needs a real drug rehab program. We aren't equipped for it. What about her withdrawals? You know she's going to have them."

"She's going to be in that medical rehab facility for a while. I imagine she'll be completely clean before they discharge her. I don't know when she'll have her trial and I don't want her anywhere near her old boyfriend. He's no good for her. If she can have a fresh start, maybe that will help her. She won't know anyone around here to go to even if she does have a weak moment." Even with all of Megan's training, she wasn't thinking with her brain—she was thinking with her heart. Helping her mother was a real option for the first time since Megan had graduated.

Since Marianne had turned her back on Gus, it was looking really good. This was Marianne's only chance at a fresh start.

Jerod rubbed his chin. "I don't think having her here will be good for the other men."

"Hold up. You said this ranch was open to women." When Megan interviewed, she had asked that very question. Jerod said if women wanted to do their rehabilitation at his ranch, he'd be happy to have both men and women. There were even separate living quarters to accommodate both sexes.

"And I do. It's not because she's a woman. Your mother hasn't proven yet that she's ready to move past her drug addiction. What happens if she gets here and has a relapse, or she brings drugs on the property and then Sam sees them? What do you think Sam is going to do?" The one thing that Jerod was very clear on was his zero-tolerance policy. The second anyone brought drugs on the ranch, they were gone. He didn't even allow anything stronger than Tylenol or Advil onsite.

Emotion was overtaking Megan's ability to reason. "She won't do that. You don't understand—she's ready. I saw her myself. The fact that she refuses to even speak to Gus tells me she's ready to move forward, finally."

"And what happens when she starts to miss Gus? Didn't she go a few months before without seeing him?"

Megan had forgotten all about her mother's last stint in rehab. Somewhere along the way Marianne had checked herself out of the halfway house and moved back in with Gus.

She sat back in her seat, feeling defeated. She understood the need to keep drugs away from the men recovering at the ranch, but Megan was certain her mom was ready to move forward.

"Are you sure you can't make room for my mom? Even if I keep a close eye on her?"

"You can't be with her twenty-four-seven. There will be times when you have to work with other patients on a one-on-one basis, and then what will your mom do? I can't keep an eye on her. She's going to have to learn to stand on her own two feet and stay clean."

"Some Christmas this is going to be," Megan mumbled.

"Megan, I want to help, I really do. I know how important family is." Jerod sat back in his chair and took a sip of his coffee. It was cooling off, so he stood up and went to top it off. "Care for more?"

Megan shook her head.

"The best I can do is give you an extended leave of absence. But I don't know how much you can do for your mom while she's in rehab." He sat back down. "Why don't you stay here and work with us like you have been until your mom is out? You can fly over every weekend or drive up Friday nights. It's not too bad of a drive. See her over the weekends and then come back here and work. At least until you know what's going to happen with her. Then, if it makes sense for you to move back to Richland to be with her, we can talk about time off."

It really was a good offer. It wasn't what she wanted, but it was fair. And of course, he was right. While she was in the hospital and then that rehab facility, there wasn't much she could do for her mother other than pray for her and be there to help wherever she could. "Alright, but I might need to go over during the week a few times if she has a court date soon. Or if I need to see her attorney."

"That's fair. I'm sure we can work something out." He stood. "I've gotta get back outside. The guys are coming back from the tree farm any minute now and I need to see to the animals."

"I'll get dinner started." Megan stood. "And Jerod, thanks. I appreciate you working with me."

"Don't thank me yet." He nodded and left the house out the back door.

Chapter 27

"It's good to have you back." Cody slapped Daniel on the back. "How's Megan doing?"

Daniel shook his head. "Not so good. I think she's gonna quit her job and move to Washington to help her mom." He slumped down at the kitchen table and hung his head.

"Sorry, man. That's rough." Cody ran his hands through his hair. "So, does this mean Megan won't be your plus-one for Christmas dinner?"

A sad, deep chuckle escaped Daniel's lips. "Are you kidding? I doubt it was ever a possibility."

"How about I pray for you two? And maybe Sunday you can speak to the preacher about it all."

"How about he asks the preacher now?" Grandpops walked in with his toothless grin, followed by the preacher himself.

Both Cody and Daniel stood up. Pastor Dunhill greeted them both with a warm smile and hearty handshakes.

"Pastor, what brings you here today? Looking to see Santa?" Cody joked, knowing even the Pastor enjoyed the fun side of the Christmas season.

"Actually, yes. We need to discuss the toy drive and I was hoping to see if we could add a couple names to the list, if it's not too late." The pastor took a seat at the kitchen table and accepted a hot mug of coffee from Cody.

The pastor was an older man in his late fifties. He looked like he'd probably had a full head of dark-brown hair in his youth, but gray seemed to have crept in from nowhere and taken root on the man's head. However, his smile gave him a youthful look, one that said he knew how to have fun as well as how to worship God. Everyone in town loved him, even those who didn't attend his church.

"Oh, don't tell me we have another farm or ranch having a rough time of it this winter?" Cody leaned back and closed his eyes.

"We do. But enough about that. What does Daniel need counsel for?" He turned his eyes toward the man in question and waited patiently, as he always did, for Daniel to speak.

Daniel cleared his throat and rubbed his chin. Then he took another sip of his coffee and looked down into the mug.

"Come on, Grandpops, let's give them some privacy." Cody tried to usher his grandfather out, but he refused to budge.

"Is this about a woman? It's always about a woman, isn't it?" Grandpops sat down at the table. "Listen here, young man, all you gotta do is say you're sorry. Doesn't matter if you were at fault or not—the woman is always right. Remember that bit of advice and life with a pretty girl will always go so much easier." He grunted and stood back up. "Oh, and bring her flowers. Not every week, but a couple times a month on different days, and after she's already thrown out the old ones." Without waiting for a reply, Joseph Makinaw left the room.

The pastor chuckled. "He's not wrong. I'd listen to a man who was happily married like he was."

"If only." Daniel snorted. "I wish it were that easy." He had already apologized. But he hadn't brought her flowers, at least not yet. However, he doubted flowers would keep Megan in town. Not when she had a chance to help her mother.

"Alright, then why don't you tell me what's eatin' at you, son?" The older man of God sat there waiting as he watched Daniel mull over what to say.

Some of what was bugging Daniel couldn't be shared with anyone. He had promised Megan he'd not gossip about her mother. On the other hand, this wasn't gossip. It was more like seeking Godly counsel. He decided he should take this chance and tell Pastor Dunhill what was bugging him. There was no way he could do the right thing all on his own—he needed Godly wisdom.

There was nothing wrong with seeking advice when he needed it.

Forty-five minutes later, Daniel walked outside with new purpose. He headed toward Cody to let him know he needed to head out to see Megan before it was too late.

Of course, Cody had no issues with his best friend doing what he needed to do, even if the man had been gone for over a week. Friendship was more important than business. And Cody even reminded him of how much time and effort Daniel had put into the tree farm trying to help him save it.

Daniel reassured himself that it was alright to leave since there were so many people there helping to run things. It all was running so nicely, and he knew that the tree farm was on its way to actually turning a profit again.

Daniel thought about what he was going to say on the entire drive over to the Crooked Arrow Ranch.

And he prayed.

By the time he exited his truck, Jerod was walking toward him with a huge grin across his face. "Are you here to help me convince Megan to stay?"

Daniel stopped in his tracks. "So she's still here?"

"For now. We had a long talk last night and I think we came up with a plan." Jerod went on to explain the weekend travel idea and possibly taking more time off when Marianne had a court date.

"That's a great idea. I spoke with Pastor Dunhill and he suggested something similar." Daniel rubbed the back of his neck. "He also had another idea, but I'm not too sure about it."

"What's that?" Jerod turned toward the house. "Hold up." He looked up at the sky. "Those dark clouds look like it's going to snow early today. Let's go inside for coffee and we'll talk there."

Once they both had a fresh cup of hot coffee in front of them to ward off the chill of the coming snowstorm, Daniel opened up.

"So, the pastor thinks that if you can offer Marianne a spot here, the courts might remand her to your care. For rehab and a chance to get away from those who are a bad influence on her." When Jerod's face went pale, Daniel winced. "Too much to ask?"

After taking a deep breath and releasing a long sigh, Jerod shook his head. "I'm sorry. Megan asked, too. But I can't do anything to risk the health and welfare of the veterans I'm here to serve."

"You don't think Marianne is ready to stay off drugs?" Even though Daniel knew what Jerod was going to say, he had to ask the question anyway.

"I think Marianne is going to say and do whatever she has to in order to keep from going to prison. She's gonna be good and stay away from Gus as long as it serves her purpose. Then, when she's in the clear, she'll go back to Gus." The ranch owner was being excruciatingly direct.

"Don't sugar-coat it. Just tell me how it is." Daniel chuckled, but he wasn't feeling it.

Jerod put his hands on the table in front of him. "Look, Daniel. I get it. You want to help Megan and her mother. I want to help, too. Believe it or not, I really do. But until Marianne does the work needed to prove she's really changed and ready to lead a clean and sober life, I can't risk any of my men here falling prey to her drugs. We always have at least one or two who struggled with some sort of addiction before coming here. I only accept recovering addicts who've done the program and put in the time to get clean and stay clean."

"I get it. I really do. But I saw Marianne for myself. I think this seizure really scared the life out of her. It might have even rewired a few brain cells to no longer need the drugs."

"Then you take her. Have her stay with you and Steve in town. Megan can go visit on a regular basis. And I'm sure some of the local women will even take her under their wing during the day. We can find a lot of ways to keep the woman busy. But it can't be here. Not yet. Not until I'm confident she won't bring any of our wounded vets down with her." Jerod took a long chug of coffee, then stared confidently into Daniel's eyes.

"I'll have to ask Uncle Steve, but it's not a bad idea. If she avoids jail time."

Jerod tilted his head. "And even if she does do some time, Marianne could still come live with you two. Can she cook?" He laughed. Everyone knew that the two bachelors could only make a basic ranch hand stew and chili. The rest of their meals were either from a restaurant or a frozen box.

"Hey, I've learned how to make a few things." Daniel gruffed and crossed his arms over his chest.

"Like I said, can she cook?" Jerod arched a brow, just daring Daniel to challenge him.

Daniel put his hands in the air. "Fine, fine. I know. But we do try."

"Crockpot meals are great, just not every day for every meal." A laugh escaped Jerod and he tried to cover his mouth.

"You're one to talk. I heard about some of the meals you've made when your cook isn't around." The entire town knew that Jerod and his guys had only survived before he got his cook because of crockpot meals. It wasn't too tough to throw a bunch of food into a pot and turn it on.

"Hey, I make great scrambled eggs and toast."

"Jerod, no you don't," a male voice admonished when he walked in the room.

"Sam, you weren't eavesdropping, were you?" Jerod stood and glared at the man.

While Sam had his faults, the man didn't try to gossip or listen in too much.

"Nah, I don't care what you two were discussing. Sounded like you were trading barbs and maybe recipes." The grouchy veteran filled his insulated travel mug with more coffee and went out back. It was his day to stay back at the ranch and help take care of the animals.

"Hey, thanks for coming over and talking to me about this. I would really appreciate it if you could find a way to keep Megan here. She's great with the men, and I think we're going to get a few lady vets come the new year. I don't know what I'd do without her." There wasn't enough time for Jerod to hire anyone new should Megan leave without at least a thirty-day notice. But he also didn't want to try and hire someone now if Megan decided to stay. And the ranch did need a full-time, live-in counselor.

"I'll see what I can do." Daniel stood to leave.

Later that night, he got down on his knees next to his bed and prayed for guidance as well as a way for Megan to stay in town. And if God would allow, for him and Megan to find a way to be together. Or at the very least, for Daniel to be Megan's friend.

His heart ached for the woman and her mother. He'd give just about anything to help them both.

Chapter 28

Everything was going smoothly with Megan taking off for two days a week and going to see her mother. She hadn't seen much of Daniel. Not after their fight. Although, that was probably more her fault than his. The cowboy tried seeing her several times, but she was too busy to talk much.

It wasn't that she was too busy, it was that she didn't want to spend time with him. After the fight she'd realized how much she cared for Daniel, and how much she had come to depend on him. Megan couldn't depend on anyone but herself, and God.

What happened when it came time for her to move to Richland? She knew she was going to be doing that just as soon as her mother was released. But she also knew it would break her heart to leave Daniel if they got any closer. Even now she could barely stand the thought of leaving him. Her heart ached for him every day. How would it be if she let him get close again?

Megan knew herself to be a strong, independent woman. But there was something about Daniel that made her want to forget all about her own personal independence and let him care for her. It was so much easier during that week he was with her in Richland.

It had been two weeks since she'd left her mother at the hospital, and the trips back and forth were starting to take their toll. Last week her mom had been moved to the high-security rehab facility. Megan thought of it more as a jail. Her mom disagreed.

"Honey," she'd said, "I've been to jail. This is more like Club Med. Don't worry about me—I'm getting great care here." Then she looked around conspiratorially. "And the food here is so much better than that hospital garbage."

Megan had laughed as she and her mom walked around the ward that first weekend. This weekend they were going to let them walk outside in the yard. Her mom needed fresh air, and the extra distance would do wonders for her recovery.

When Megan arrived, she was surprised to see her mom's attorney there as well. It was a Saturday morning. Didn't most lawyers play golf or take out their yachts on the weekends? "Mom, Mr. Jarvis—what's going on?"

"Please, Miss Anderson, take a seat. I have some good news." Mr. Jarvis stood and motioned to a chair next to him. He was seated on the other side of her mother's hospital bed while her mom lay down looking doubtful.

"Okay." With the attorney proclaiming good news but her mom looking unsure, Megan wasn't quite sure how to feel. "What's the good news? And is there bad as well?"

Once she was seated, the attorney looked at her. The man was in his early thirties from the looks of the few lines on his face. His light-brown mustache needed a trim, but wasn't too overgrown. And his blond hair was touching the top of his shirt collar, so Megan guessed he was in need of a barber. Maybe he had even skipped an appointment with the man to be here and help her mom.

Megan looked into Mr. Jarvis's gray eyes and relaxed at the soft look he returned to her. He wasn't a bad-looking man, but he certainly wasn't cowboy material. Not with his short, slight frame and nasally voice. But he did have a caring look to him. She wondered if he was married or even had a girlfriend. What kind of woman would like her man to work Saturdays?

"Now, Miss Anderson…" he began.

"Please, call me Megan."

"Alright, Megan." Jason Jarvis didn't offer the use of his first name. "I had a very productive meeting with the district attorney late yesterday. He's inclined to offer a deal to your mother, but if she even thinks of bending it in the slightest then she'll do real prison time."

Megan gulped. This was it—her mom's chance to show everyone she had changed and make something of her life. "What's the deal?"

Jason pulled the file out of his briefcase and scanned the first page. "Besides never doing drugs again"—he stared at Marianne —"you must also agree to never see Gus, and you must leave Richland."

"Is that it?" Megan smiled and realized this might be easier than she'd thought.

"No, your mother has to do six months in a rehab facility and then three months in a halfway house. I have a list of facilities in other states that the DA has heard good things about." Mr Jarvis looked up from his file to Megan. "You live in Montana, right?"

She nodded.

He thumbed through a few pages. "Yes, right." He turned the sheet around to show Megan. "There is a facility that has the rehab program and partners with a halfway house only a few miles away. Have you heard of Helena?"

Megan grinned. "Of course. It's the capital of Montana."

"The facility is only about thirty minutes away from Helena, near a lake. The pictures look very peaceful. This facility would get Marianne away from her harmful friends, and have her close to you. Would you be amenable to having her nearby?" Handing the file to Marianne, Mr. Jarvis turned back to Megan for her answer.

"Yes, I'd like that very much." Megan looked to her mother. "Mom?"

"Hmm?" She was looking at the pictures of the facility and the area. "Oh, sorry. This place looks like a dream vacation spot."

"Would you like to live near me? Depending on exactly where the facility is, it's about two and a half to three hours from me." Electricity zinged up her spine. Her mom would be close by and not have to do hard time. This was so much more than she had prayed for. God was good.

Marianne chewed at her lower lip. "This sounds too good to be true. There's always a catch."

"You will have to submit to drug testing, stay clean, and like I said, never come back to Richland unless you have to appear before a judge. The DA doesn't want you here." It sounded like Mr. Jarvis was about to take it one step further and declare Marianne was persona non grata, but he didn't.

"Anything else?" Megan too felt it was too easy. Would he have made it this easy for them?

The sound of a cough escaping Mr. Jarvis alerted Megan to the coming bomb.

What he said next sent a shock through both the Anderson women. Megan doubted her mom would do it. And after a few minutes of silence, she decided it would be the best thing for her mother.

"You want me to rat out Gus? The man I've been with for the past ten years? The man who's taken care of me no matter what?" Marianne shook her head. She crossed her arms over her chest and glared at Mr. Jarvis.

"Mom, it really is the best thing." Megan bit her lower lip, just like her mom did. For years she had wondered where she'd picked up that bad habit. Now she knew. "He's not taken good care of you. He's led you down a dark path. Until you met him, you rarely did hard drugs. He's the one who got you into meth. He's done nothing but use you."

"But he loves me." A small tear fell down Marianne's cheek.

"No, he uses you. Just like he uses other women…and girls." A hardness covered Mr. Jarvis's face as he pulled another file out of his briefcase.

"Do we want to see this?" A trickle of fear and uncertainty spiked down Megan's spine.

Mr. Jarvis looked from the manila folder in his hand to Marianne and then to Megan. "You may not. But I think Marianne needs to know who Gus really is."

After a moment's hesitation, Marianne wiped the tear from her face and pursed her lips. Then she held out her hand.

Wordlessly, the folder passed from Mr. Jarvis to Marianne. She put it in her lap for a moment and stared at it.

"Mom, if you don't want to, I can and then tell you about it."

"No." Marianne paused. "I need to see this for myself."

The first photo wasn't too shocking. It was of Gus holding a middle-aged woman against him. From the looks of it, he was about to kiss her. The woman looked haggard but interested.

It was the second photo that had both Marianne and Megan wishing they hadn't looked. Gus had stacks of money on a table sitting next to bags of drugs. Megan wasn't an expert or anything, but from the looks of it there had to be close to a million dollars on the table.

Marianne closed the folder and handed it back to Mr. Jarvis, ignoring the rest of the photos. "I had no idea. He always said we were barely making it. How could he have that much while we lived in squalor? I mean, there were rats in the building! I had to live with rats while he handled millions."

"From what we can tell, he's only a low-level dealer for a much larger drug dealer. This is why the DA wanted to prosecute you so badly. But when I spoke to him and told him you couldn't have known about this, he came up with the plan for you to tell the courts what you do know." The folder went back into Mr. Jarvis's briefcase, never to be seen again by Megan or Marianne.

"That much money and drugs, it has to be cartel-related, doesn't it?" Fear entered Marianne's eyes and she shrank back into her bed.

The idea struck Megan like lightning, and she worried for her mother. "Will she be safe if she tells the DA what she knows?"

"If need be she can go into witness protection, but I doubt your mother knows anything other than what Gus was up to. Guys like this don't even know which cartel they work for. There's probably at least three, maybe even four layers between Gus and the leaders. But if the state can get Gus then they might be able to get to the next guy, and so on and so forth. It's a long way off, but at the very least this one dealer will be off the streets for good."

"How'd you get those photos?" Now Megan was thinking strategically. If they had this sort of evidence, what did they need her mother for?

"A raid at a rival gang's headquarters earlier this week provided a lot of information. Not only against Gus, but others. A very big drug war is in the making here and everyone wants to stop it before anyone innocent gets hurt." After checking the time, Mr. Jarvis stood up. "Think about it. I'll be back on Monday to get your answer."

Of course, the answer was yes.

Chapter 29

M onday afternoon saw Daniel selling trees at the farm. They were swamped. It was one week until Christmas, and those who hadn't picked up trees yet were scrambling to get good ones.

"Merry Christmas. I hope you enjoy your tree." Daniel grinned and waved as the family of five hauled the tree to their vehicle. He loved the smell of Christmas; the different pine scents always mixed perfectly at the tree farm. And then when he added in the cinnamon from the various treats they sold in the little barn where he had his cash register, he couldn't help but smile all day.

Before Daniel went to help the next family, he looked outside the window and saw the small snowflakes falling to the ground, creating a light layer of fluffy white snow. It was so perfect it almost looked fake, like in those Christmas shows. Except this wasn't fake, it was the real stuff and glittered when lights hit the snow just right.

He had been so busy, he didn't even notice that Megan was standing off to the side of the register and waiting patiently for him to finish his line of customers. When the last one had paid for their tree and garland, Daniel noticed the look of worry on Megan's face and he locked his register before heading to her.

"Hey, is everything all right?" His arms went up to pull her to him but he stopped himself. They hadn't spoken much the past two weeks and he wasn't exactly sure if she would welcome a hug from him or not.

Megan didn't seem to think about it; she barreled into his arms and buried her head in his chest. "I'm so sorry."

"What for?" Without any thought at all, Daniel's arms went around Megan and he held her tight. Her scent enveloped him and he lost track of all sound. He felt like he was in a bubble of vanilla and peppermint with a hint of cinnamon. All of his favorite scents, besides the Christmas pine tree scent.

"I never should have pushed you away."

"Shh, it's alright. I'm here. What happened?" He leaned over and kissed the top of her head.

"So much. I don't even know where to start. Can you get away so we can talk?" She pulled her head back and looked up at him with a tear-streaked face.

The need he saw in her eyes hit Daniel straight in his chest.

Cody walked up right then and took one look at them and motioned for Daniel to leave. "I've got this. Don't worry."

"Thanks, man. I appreciate it." Daniel took Megan by the arms and walked her to the barn where they had their small employee breakroom.

"Mrs. Claus, I'm not sure your plan for those two is working." Santa rubbed his bearded chin and watched Megan and Daniel walk away.

"My darling Santa, don't you know that it's times like this that the Lord steps in and helps couples find the true love they're destined for? All you need is a little faith." Mrs. Claus patted her husband's hand and they walked away.

No one else was in the breakroom, so Daniel closed the door and offered Megan a chair and a cup of hot cocoa. "Sorry, it looks as though we're out of coffee in here. But if you want a mug of coffee I can go locate some."

"No, don't leave. Cocoa will be perfect." A tentative smile turned up the corners of Megan's mouth, but didn't reach her eyes.

Outside, the sounds of the carnival music pierced the silence in the room and Daniel thought how strange it was to hear the upbeat music while Megan looked so sad. "Rudolph the Red-Nosed Reindeer" began to play when she looked at him.

"It's good news, in a way. But my mom could be in danger. I don't know how she missed the signs, and how I missed them, too. Although, I did my best to avoid their apartment and Gus as much as I could over the past ten years." Megan took a long swig of the cocoa and winced when the hot drink hit her throat.

"Hey, slow down. Tell me what's happened." He took the drink out of her hands and put it on the table in front of her, then took a seat next to her and held both of her hands in his.

And Megan told him the entire story—everything they knew about Gus and the deal her mom had made earlier that day with the district attorney.

The heaviness of everything that Megan had been dealing with hit him like a ton of bricks, and he regretted taking a step back. He never should have let her push him away and he knew it. Without a word, he scooted his chair as close to her as he could and wrapped her in his arms.

After a few heavy moments, he knew what to say for a change. "At least your mom will be close and you won't have to leave. She'll be safe in Helena. Just you wait and see."

"This has turned out to be one strange Christmas, hasn't it?" She chuckled and took a deep breath.

"Yes, but it has brought us closer. I don't know if it's too soon, but would you have dinner with me one night this week?" He'd done it. Daniel had asked her out. He only hoped he hadn't put his boot in his mouth again.

Turned out, it was the perfect thing to say.

Megan pulled away from him and smiled. It was the sort of smile of that went from ear to ear and reached her eyes. She even had a sparkle. "Are you asking me out on a proper date?"

Relief flooded him. Daniel returned her grin. "Yes, I am. I know we've been out to eat plenty of times together, but in the past it was only two friends sharing a meal. This time I want a real date."

Two nights later, Daniel drove to the Crooked Arrow Ranch and walked up the porch steps. He noticed that the front of the ranch house could use a new coat of paint, and the porch swing had seen better days.

Jerod answered the door after Daniel rang the bell. When he opened the door to let Daniel inside, he led them to the dining room table where Jerod had set up two shotguns, ammunition was strewn on the table, and cleaning supplies sat there. When Jerod sat down, he picked up one of the shotguns and a rag and started wiping oil on the outside of the barrel. "I'll have you know that Megan's an important part of this here ranch and I won't stand for any man, even you, hurting her." He put the gun down and glared at Daniel.

If Daniel didn't know Jerod like he did, he would have been afraid for his life and maybe even run out of there screaming. He felt sorry for any boys who dated Jerod's future daughters. The man had intimidation down. Must have come from his Army days. Daniel still didn't know exactly what Jerod did, other than he was in special forces at some point.

Daniel had to bite the inside of his cheek to keep from grinning. But the moment Megan showed up, all thoughts of laughing and joking fled. Figgy pudding, all thoughts period fled his brain. Megan was gorgeous in a long wool red dress with a white collar. She looked like a young Mrs. Claus, or one of those models who sold perfume at Christmas.

Her sandy brown hair was curled and styled to show her high cheekbones and bright eyes. His stomach did somersaults, and if he could have thought he would have known he was in trouble. This woman had just stolen his heart and he was never going to get it back.

She smiled at him and looked him up and down. Daniel had worn black boots, jeans, and a hat. His shirt matched hers with the Christmas red. Megan walked up to him and kissed his cheek. "Merry Christmas, cowboy."

"Merry, merry Christmas." Daniel returned her cheek-kiss and took her hand.

Jerod walked them to the door and broke the bubble that Daniel and Megan were living in when he warned him, "I expect to see her back here at a decent hour, and she better not be crying." He held up his other shotgun, the one that still needed to be cleaned.

The glare Jerod gave Daniel caused him to stand taller. "Yes, sir."

As Daniel walked Megan to his truck, he looked back over his shoulder and caught Jerod giving him the evil eye. He thought to himself, *I can't wait for this guy to get married. Then he'll be too busy with his new wife to bother us.*

<h1 style="text-align:center">Epilogue</h1>

C hristmas Day was much more special than anyone in Frenchtown could have expected. All of the kids were taken care of by Santa and his secret elves. Not a single family in the area went without a hot ham or turkey dinner for the special day. And the snow was falling lightly, just enough to make a perfect picture but not enough to cause any problems on the highway as the local residents went from home to home to visit family and friends.

Santa and Mrs. Claus stopped by the Crooked Arrow Ranch to visit their latest couple.

"See, Santa. I told you Daniel and Megan would figure it all out. All you needed was a little faith." Mrs. Claus wrapped her hand around her husband's and sighed.

"Yes, yes. You're always right when it comes to matchmaking. But the stress of watching them mess things up along the way always causes me heartburn. What do you say next year, you let someone else take over the role of Christmas matchmaker?"

Mrs. Claus lightly chuckled. "We shall see. We shall see, my dear."

The Christmas couple sighed as they watched Daniel point to the ball of mistletoe above Megan's head.

"Hey, that wasn't there earlier. Who did this?" Megan looked around. "Jerod wouldn't have, that's for sure. He still gives you the evil eye if you kiss my cheek."

Daniel shrugged. "Wasn't me, but I sure plan on taking advantage." He leaned in and put his thumb under Megan's chin. When he lifted it, she complied and her lips touched his. The kiss began sweet and slow, but as time went on their lips parted and the kiss naturally went to the next step.

Mrs. Claus sighed. "Always keep a sprig of mistletoe in the truck, Santa. You never know when it's going to be needed."

So, what did you think? Wanna read more about the Crooked Arrow Ranch and the wounded vets who find healing, and on occasion, Love? Then keep an eye out for my newest series, Crooked Arrow Ranch.

While you're waiting, join my mailing list and get the prequel free. Wounded Hearts Ranch is about how Jerod and Dana met and got together.

<h1 style="text-align:center">Author's Notes</h1>

Wow, this story took a turn I wasn't expecting. I hope you enjoyed the detours along the way to seeing Daniel and Megan finding their happily ever after. When I began writing this book, I had planned on doing more of the fun Christmas stuff, like in earlier books of this series, and also maybe even a little bit like my Miss Claus series (in my J.L. Hendricks pen name), but stuff happened.

I don't want to get all serious, but when America pulled out of Afghanistan, and left so many of our people behind, I was hurt and angry. As a US Army Veteran, I have a great respect for our military and what they do. Especially in the Middle East. Then, as I watched how the US Media and prominent people began turning their backs on our military, I was even more angry. I had to show that our vets deserve our respect, not hatred.

When a soldier comes back from the Middle East, it's not the same as traditional warfare. Not anymore. I only touched on the topic of PTSD in this book. It is a Christmas story, so I couldn't go into too much detail. But my next series will probably be the most emotional series I've written to date. It will be my love story to all of our military heroes, those who've come home and those who haven't.

I hope you'll join me and read the Crooked Arrow Ranch series. And remember, thank a veteran for your freedom. While we may not always agree with the war, or conflicts our politicians put us in, it is the troops who protect the people. Without our troops, monsters like Napoleon or Hitler, would rule the world.

It's been over a year since I first planned the Crooked Arrow Ranch, which was before the pull out from Afghanistan. I even wrote a short story last Christmas that was included with a multi-author Anthology. Once I got the story back from the anthology, I held onto it, waiting for the time when I could start the new series. Christmas 2021 is when I will launch the first book.

It will take place on the Crooked Arrow Ranch in Frenchtown, Montana. So many of the characters from the Big Sky Christmas series will be in it, including Lottie and her Frenchtown Roasting Company. In case you haven't figured it out yet, I love a great coffee drink paired with the perfect pastry.

Speaking of which, I have a special coffee recipe included. I want to say a special thank you to my friend, Julie, who gave me the recipe and allowed me to share it with everyone who picks up a copy of this book. Keep reading for the delicious Pumpkin Spice Latte that Daniel loved so much!

This Christmas, let's all pray for peace on Earth and good will toward man, as well as for revival all over the world. God really is the only one who can heal our hearts and souls.

Remember, *For God so loved the world that he gave His one and only begotten Son, that whosoever shall believe on him, shall not perish, but have eternal life.*

Pumpkin Spice Latte (PSL)

16 oz mug or cup

5 pumps of Pumpkin Spice syrup directly into your cup

Pour 4 shots of espresso into the cup

Stir the mixture a bit

Foam your milk. Julie uses ½ and ½ for a creamier froth. Takes about 1.5 mins, depending on your machine. (be sure to follow the direction on your machine since so many are different).

Mix the coffee, syrup, and milk as you pour it in the cup. Hold back as much of the foam as you can. I use a large spoon over the top of the frothing mug to keep it from pouring into the mug. Then, when your cup is almost full, use the spoon to top off your dink with the froth, or foam.

Sprinkle cinnamon sugar on top and enjoy!

For those of you who love social media, here are the various ways to follow or contact me:

BookBub: https://www.bookbub.com/authors/jenna-hendricks

Instagram: https://www.instagram.com/j.l.hendricks/

Twitter: https://twitter.com/TinkFan25

Facebook: https://www.facebook.com/people/JL-Hendricks/100011419945971

Website: https://jennahendricks.com

TikTok: https://www.tiktok.com/@jennacleanauthor

Free short story when you join my newsletter

https://jennahendricks.com/newsletter/

Wounded Hearts Ranch

By Jenna Hendricks

Jerod's war wounds are more than skin deep. Will he allow Dana to get close enough to heal his wounded heart?

Chapter 1

Jerod Stevens stood tall and proud as he watched his new sign, Crooked Arrow Ranch, be raised onto its post. He'd only owned the place for a few months, but he'd jumped out of the shoot faster than a raging bull trying to buck its rider in less than seven seconds. In fact, his ranch wasn't ready for anyone when his first seven residents joined him right before Christmas.

They had lost their housing when a fire ravaged the building. When the Home for a Warrior coordinator called Jerod, he was more than willing to change his Christmas plans and help out with a place to stay for Christmas. Turned out to be a lot more fun than he'd thought possible. Sure, there were some sour faces when he met them at the airport, but all in all they had a great time. Especially when he pulled out the Frenchtown Roasting Company's coffee and pastries. But what really put a smile on his new residents' faces was the Christmas breakfast—cinnamon rolls that curled the toes. They were so sweet, yet perfectly doughy.

Jerod was in love.

Not with a woman, although a certain barista at the coffee shop was quite beautiful. He was in love with the pastries. He had decided to make it a weekly tradition, and so every Sunday morning a tray of cinnamon rolls along with a vat of that week's special roast coffee waited for him at the Frenchtown Roasting Company.

A screeching sound brought him out of his reverie, and he looked around for what had made the noise that caused him to duck and cover behind the signage truck without even realizing what he had done. The noise, high-pitched and sounding like an RPG, caused his heart to race and sweat to form on his brow even though snow covered the ground and it couldn't be any warmer than thirty degrees out.

When the crunch of metal on metal hit his ears, he straightened up and ran to the two trucks. As he ran, his feet slipped and slid across the icy road. Of course, he should have realized that the road was going to be icy. Yesterday the sun came out for a few hours and melted away patches of snow. Then last night it got below freezing, and the mercury hadn't risen much since. Jerod put his arms out to balance himself as he continued forward.

The guys working on his sign followed him.

When Jerod arrived at the old red truck, he saw a young woman at the steering wheel, not moving. Her head was down on the steering wheel, as it was too old to have airbags. "Miss, can you hear me?" He pulled open the door with ease. While she had hit someone head-on, her old truck was like a tank—solid, and could take a beating without much damage.

When she still didn't move, he touched her shoulder and felt the cold permeating her being. For a moment he wondered if she was still alive. Then she stirred and moaned.

Prologue

Prologue

Harir, Iraq,

"See the columns at the top? How they are marked by the alphabet? Then on the side is a number." The blonde-haired Army officer spoke to the four local women taking his class via an interpreter. While he had picked up some Arabic, he did not know the local Kurdish language other than hi and thank you.

He was stationed in the Kurdish province of Northern Iraq on a joint US base filled with men and women from various branches of the US service. They even had the occasional squads come in from other countries to train with the US troops.

Captain Anthony Sullivan, known to his friends as Tony, stood in front of a small group of local women whom he'd been teaching to use a computer as well as how to budget for their household. With the war, so many women had been left to fend for their families while their men were either dead, or fighting. Some of the women he'd taught were married to the very men he was fighting against. But these women didn't get much choice when it came to who they married.

In Iraq, women were treated more like chattel to buy and sell than as the women the men married, or who were their mothers, daughters, and sisters. Tony worried about the women left behind and with the permission of his commander, he had begun teaching the local women how to financially care for their families. And if he got in a lesson or two about God, and his love of all human beings, then so much the better.

The local Internet café had agreed to let him use their computers to train the women for a fee. It seemed that American money went a long way in Kurdistan.

Tony never turned his back to the front door. He kept an eagle eye out for trouble, as did the Internet Café owner who liked the Americans. So when Tony heard some yelling outside the café, where he always had two guards stationed, he knew trouble was brewing.

The women ignored the shouts, as it was a regular occurrence in their part of the world. At times, it sounded as though someone was about to start fighting, when in reality they were just haggling for some deal, or other. But Tony knew the difference, especially when his radio squawked a code word – Rain.

"Alright, let's get to the back of the building." Tony knew the back had an emergency exit, but it was most likely blocked by the recent shipment Kalid had received for his shop. Cursing under his breath, Tony tried to get all the women to safety before the fighting began.

The women, for their part, did quite well. They were chatting in their own local dialect, so he didn't understand them, but he could tell from the way their eyes squinted they weren't afraid, just frustrated. The local Kurdish women rarely wore the black head coverings, or hajib, that covered most of their face. Kurdish women let their faces be seen. The one thing that Tony appreciated the most about the Kurdish culture, they didn't want to hide their women behind black. Instead, the women chose to wear colorful long flowing dresses that made the women beautiful and feminine, not looking like they were wearing black potato sacks.

Sounds of gunfire whistled through the air and Tony knew they were in the middle of trouble. He placed himself between the women and the front door. "Quick, get these boxes out of the way." Tony pointed to the pile of boxes and crates that covered part of the back door and the interpreter translated for him.

The front door burst open and a man wearing all black, and a vest laden with plastic explosives, probably stolen from a US base, began yelling in Arabic. He obviously wasn't Kurdish, and he most likely wasn't even from this part of Iraq. Unfortunately, none of that mattered at the moment. All that mattered was getting everyone out of the café before the suicide bomber made good on his threat to blow them all to hell.

It was amazing what went through Tony's mind as he realized he wasn't going to leave here alive. He prayed that the women would survive, and that the men and women in his squad outside would be alright.

Tony faced the man standing in the entrance and put his hands up. "Please, don't hurt the women. They only wanted to learn how to manage their household finances while their husbands were away. They did nothing wrong." He tried to convey as best he could his request in Arabic.

Several ideas quickly entered his mind on ways to talk the bomber down, but when he looked into the eyes of the man whose hand was on a kill switch, he knew there was nothing that could be done. The anger and steely determination glaring back at him sent shivers down his spine.

"Allahu akbar!" the man screamed before he moved his thumb off the plunger of the detonator.

Tony turned to the right and tried to get behind the table that had been overturned, but he was too late. The last thing Tony saw was a bright light and he prayed God would be waiting for him on the other side.

Chapter 1

Chapter 1

"Hope, we can't thank you enough for agreeing to come and help us out." Annie Baker pulled her niece in for a hug. "This means the world to us."

"Can't...breathe..." Hope feigned as she returned her aunt's hug. It wasn't that the hug was too tight, it was that she felt awkward with all of the gratitude. Truth be told, she was the one who should be grateful. If she had to stay home one more week she was going to commit hari kari, or something worse - like take her ex back.

Annie pulled back and smiled from ear to ear. "Oh, sweetheart." She pinched Hope's cheek and sighed. "It's going to be nice having another woman around. Your Uncle Jesse and the two ranch hands we have aren't the same as having a woman to talk with."

Heat began making its way up Hope's neck and into her cheeks. She couldn't believe all of the fuss about her coming to help her aunt and uncle on their farm. The moment Dana had come home from her honeymoon, Hope called Dana and asked to come and visit. Hope and Dana had been close cousins, until this past year. They had spent summers visiting each other and kept in touch all year long.

While Hope had been at the wedding, she was only there as a guest, and didn't get to see much of her cousin. And when she watched Dana walk down that aisle, Hope realized how much she had missed out on while she was under the spell of that scoundrel.

The only reason Hope wasn't a bride's maid was because she had been too wrapped up in an unhealthy relationship. When it finally went sideways, and Hope reached out to her cousin, Dana had already picked out her bridesmaids. Hope really regretted ignoring her cousin all those months. But she knew that if Dana heard her voice, she'd know exactly what Hope had been up to, hence the radio silence on her part. The last thing she wanted was her cousin finding out what she'd been doing.

So, when Aunt Annie invited her to come and help at their farm, she jumped at the chance to renew her closeness with her cousin who was more like a sister, than a cousin. Hope had been at the Baker Farm for only three days, but she'd seen Dana twice already. And they had plans to go out to dinner that night, just the two of them.

"Really, Aunt Annie. I'm so glad to be here. You know how much I love you and Uncle Jesse. And this ranch." A sense of belonging hit Hope right in the chest, and she knew she'd made the right choice. It wasn't that there was anything wrong with her family or their ranch, she just needed a change. And this was the perfect place to get her head screwed back on straight. And her heart right.

"Remember that one summer when you were here? I think you and Dana were about twelve. You two had a running bet all summer long on who'd win the most races." Annie leaned back and looked off into the distance remembering when the girls were younger, and a smile inched its way across her lips. "Those were the best summers."

"I agree. I always loved coming here and having Dana over to my ranch." Hope giggled when a distant memory came back.

"What's so funny?" A line Hope couldn't remember seeing on her aunt's forehead stood out prominently before her brows moved together in confusion.

Hope rubbed her nose, trying to hide her grin. "Oh, nothing." It was something, but she didn't want to rat out her cousin.

Annie put her hands on her hips and pursed her lips. "Out with it."

Hope never could defy her aunt when she gave her that look. Hope felt the disappointment in her aunt's glare and the last thing she wanted was for her aunt to be upset with her. Even as a kid, she never wanted her aunt to be mad at her. Now her mother…well, that was another story. But Aunt Annie was the adult she always looked up to and confided in growing up.

With a sigh, Hope quirked her lips to the side and nodded. "Well, I guess it won't hurt now. Dana is married and not living here anymore." Hope looked around and lowered her voice, as though she was about to convey a state secret. "When Dana came to see me one summer, we were thirteen and just starting to like boys." She stopped and covered her mouth, trying to stifle a giggle.

"Oh, please don't tell me that my Dana was caught kissing a ranch hand." Annie looked to the sky and shook her head, almost regretting what was to come.

"Not quite." The boy she caught her cousin with wasn't exactly a ranch hand. "James was the son of the ranch foreman. And I walked in on them making out in the hay loft." Hope giggled with the memory. James had turned out to be pretty wild. She should have known he would be. The rest of the summer, he'd been caught with two other girls around town, and the boy wasn't even old enough to drive yet. But, he did have that cowboy swagger down pat.

Annie laughed. The kind of laugh that drew a snort and caused her cheeks to turn pink with embarrassment. "Oh, my. Please tell me James and you never went out?"

Hope waved a hand before her face. "Please, James turned out to be the town player before he even graduated high school." She grinned. "And besides, Dana and I had a motto, sisters before misters. We always stuck to that. If she liked a boy, I never even gave him a second look, even after she left. And if I liked one, she would always investigate him." Hope wished Dana had been there when she met her ex. Things would have been so much better if she'd never fallen under his spell.

"Sooo…" Annie looked at her niece out of the corner of her eye. "Did you leave anyone special back home?"

Hope snorted. "Goodness, no." She shook her head. "I've sworn off men. I need to focus on helping you and Uncle Jesse get back on track since Dana left you high and dry for a man!" She shivered, knowing good and well that Dana did whatever she could to help her parents out in addition to working at the local coffee shop and helping her new husband at his own ranch.

Annie sniffed and pretended to swipe a tear from under eye. "I don't know what we would have done without you, dear." But she couldn't hold the charade up for long and a smile crept up her lips before she started laughing outright.

"It feels like I'm home, you know?" Little lines indented between Hope's brows, and she pursed her lips. "I know I have a home with my parents, but this place, this town, has always felt special." She shrugged and shook her head. "I don't know if I'm saying it right, but I love his place as though it was my own home."

Annie pulled her niece in for another hug. "Dear, this is your home. And it always will be. Our door is open to you no matter what. And we've never changed your room." She pulled back and a sly smile began. "Now, Dana's room. That's a different story."

Both laughed thinking about how Annie had already begun making changes to Dana's childhood room. Since Dana had married and moved to the Crooked Arrow Ranch with her new husband, Jerod, Annie had plans to turn the space into her own personal sewing room.

"Do you think I can take a corner of the room and set up my crafts?" Hope grinned, knowing full well that she rarely had time to craft. Most of her free time was spent on horseback. In fact, she looked down at her watch and winced when she realized how late it was. She had a date.

Pick up Hope's Healing Love

Pick up your copy of Hope's Healing Love today wherever paperback books are sold. If you don't see it in your favorite store, or library, please ask that this book be included today.

And join Hope and Tony as they find the peace they are looking for, as well a love that heals.